SPECIAL MESSAGE TO READERS

THE ULVERSCROFT FOUNDATION

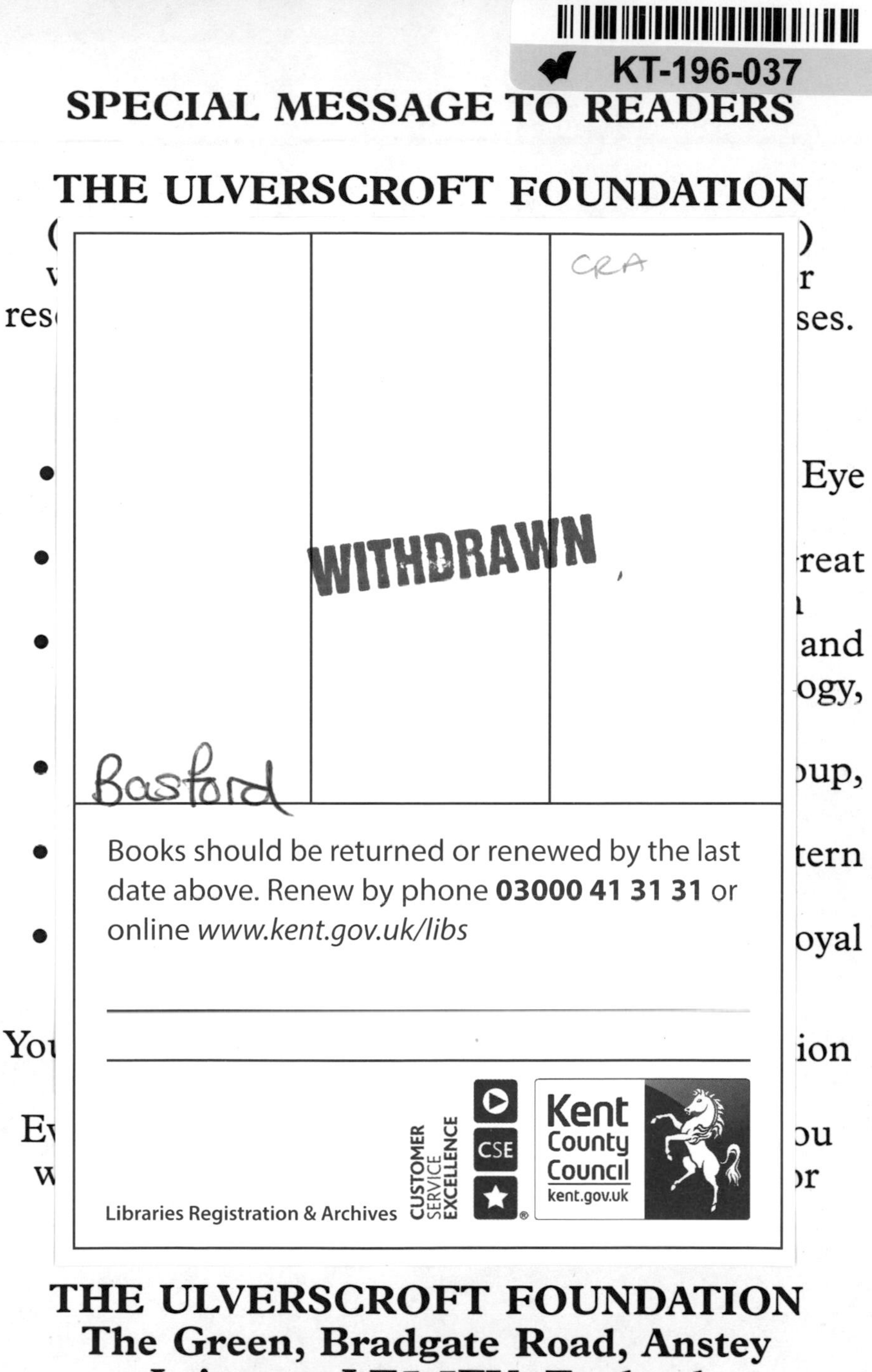

THE ULVERSCROFT FOUNDATION
The Green, Bradgate Road, Anstey
Leicester LE7 7FU, England
Tel: (0116) 236 4325

website: www.foundation.ulverscroft.com

THE FURTHER ADVENTURES OF MR. VERDANT GREEN
an Oxford Freshman

Having emerged from his baptism of fire as an Oxford Freshman, Mr. Verdant Green returns to the University, (endearingly) optimistic, (somewhat) experienced, and (very slightly) less credulous. Gleefully ready to hoax the new student blood in his turn, he fancies himself now a man of the world, wise in the ways of college life. Yet, despite his status as a veteran of one term, our hero still finds himself no less vulnerable to fetching up in scrapes — occasioned by overambitious horses, oversized cigars, and pugilistic conflicts between Town and Gown . . .

Books by Cuthbert Bede
Published by Ulverscroft:

THE ADVENTURES OF
MR. VERDANT GREEN

MR. VERDANT GREEN, MARRIED
AND DONE FOR

CUTHBERT BEDE

THE FURTHER ADVENTURES OF MR. VERDANT GREEN

an Oxford Freshman

Complete and Unabridged

ULVERSCROFT
Leicester

First published in Great Britain in 1854

This Large Print Edition
published 2016

A catalogue record for this book is available from the British Library.

ISBN 978–1–4448–2720–0

Published by
F. A. Thorpe (Publishing)
Anstey, Leicestershire

Set by Words & Graphics Ltd.
Anstey, Leicestershire
Printed and bound in Great Britain by
T. J. International Ltd., Padstow, Cornwall

This book is printed on acid-free paper

Contents

1

Mr. Verdant Green Recommences his Existence as an Oxford Undergraduate

The intelligent reader — which epithet I take to be a synonym for every one who has perused the first part of the Adventures of Mr. Verdant Green — will remember the statement, that the hero of the narrative 'had gained so much experience during his Freshman's term, that, when the pleasures of the Long Vacation were at an end, and he had returned to Brazenface with his firm and fast friend Charles Larkyns, he felt himself entitled to assume a patronizing air to the Freshmen, who then entered, and even sought to impose upon their credulity in ways which his own personal experience suggested.' And the intelligent reader will further call to mind the fact that the first part of these memoirs concluded with the words — 'it was clear that Mr. Verdant Green had made his farewell bow as an Oxford Freshman.'

But, although Mr. Verdant Green had of

necessity ceased to be 'a Freshman' as soon as he had entered upon his second term of residence, — the name being given to students in their first term only, — yet this necessity, which, as we all know, *non habet leges*, will occasionally prove its rule by an exception; and if Mr. Verdant Green was no longer a Freshman in name, he still continued to be one by nature. And the intelligent reader will perceive when he comes to study these veracious memoirs, that, although their hero will no longer display those peculiarly virulent symptoms of freshness, which drew towards him so much friendly sympathy during the earlier part of his University career, yet that he will still, by his innocent simplicity and credulity, occasionally evidence the truth of the Horatian maxim —

'Quo semel est imbuta recens, servabit odorem
Testa diu;'

which, when *Smart*-ly translated, means, 'A cask will long preserve the flavour, with which, when new, it was once impregnated;' and which, when rendered in the Saxon vulgate, signifieth, 'What is bred in the bone will come out in the flesh.'

It would, indeed, take more than a

Freshman's term, — a two months' residence in Oxford, — to remove the simple gaucheries of the country Squire's hobbodehoy, and convert the girlish youth, the pupil of that Nestor of Spinsters, Miss Virginia Verdant, into the MAN whose school was the University, whose Alma Mater was Oxonia herself. We do not cut our wise teeth in a day; some people, indeed, are so unfortunate as never to cut them at all; at the best, two months is but a brief space in which to get through this sapient teething operation, a short time in which to graft our cutting on the tree of Wisdom, more especially when the tender plant happens to be a Verdant Green. The golden age is past when the full-formed goddess of Wisdom sprang from the brain of Jove complete in all her parts. If our Vulcans now-a-days were to trepan the heads of our Jupiters, they would find nothing in them! In these degenerate times it will take more than one splitting headache to produce *our* wisdom.

So it was with our hero. The splitting headache, for example, which had wound up the pleasures of Mr. Small's 'quiet party,' had taught him that the good things of this life were not given to be abused, and that he could not exceed the bounds of temperance and moderation without being made to pay the penalty of the trespass. It had taught him that kind of wisdom which even 'makes fools wise'; for it had taught him Experience. And yet, it was but a portion of that lesson of Experience which it is sometimes so hard to learn, but which, when once got by heart, is like the catechism of our early days, — it is never forgotten, — it directs us, it warns us, it advises us; it not only adorns the tale of our life, but it points the moral which may bring that tale to a happy and peaceful end.

Experience! Experience! What will it not do? It is a staff which will help us on when we are jostled by the designing crowds of our Vanity Fair. It is a telescope that will reveal to us the dark spots on what seemed to be a fair face. It is a finger-post to show us whither the crooked paths of worldly ways will lead us. It is a scar that tells of the wound which the soldier has received in the battle of life. It is a lighthouse that warns us off those hidden rocks and quicksands where the wrecks of long past joys that once smiled so fairly, and were loved so dearly, now lie buried in all their ghastliness, stripped of grace and beauty, things to shudder at and dread. Experience! Why, even Alma Mater's doctors prescribe it to be taken in the largest quantities! 'Experientia — *dose it*!' they say: and very largely some of us have to pay for the dose. But the dose does us good; and (for it is an allopathic remedy), the greater the dose, the greater is the benefit to be derived.

The two months' allopathic dose of Experience, which had been administered to Mr. Verdant Green, chiefly through the agency of those skilful professors, Messrs. Larkyns, Fosbrooke, Smalls, and Bouncer, had been so far beneficial to him, that, in the figurative Eastern language of the last-named gentleman, he had not only been 'sharpened up no end by being well rubbed against University bricks,' but he had, moreover, 'become so considerably wide-awake, that he would very soon be able to take the shine out of the old original Weazel, whom the pages of History had recorded as never having been discovered in a state of somnolence.'

Now, as Mr. Bouncer was a gentleman of considerable experience and was, too, (although addicted to expressions not to be found in 'the Polite Preceptor,') quite free from the vulgar habit of personal flattery, — or, as he thought fit to express it, in words which would have taken away my Lord Chesterfield's appetite, 'buttering a party to his face in the cheekiest manner,' — we may fairly presume on this strong evidence, that Mr. Verdant Green had really gained a considerable amount of experience during his

Freshman's term, although there were still left in his character and conduct many marks of viridity which

'Time's effacing fingers,'

assisted by Mr. Bouncer's instructions, would gradually remove. However, Mr. Verdant Green had, at any rate, ceased to be 'a Freshman' in name; and had received that University promotion, which Mr. Charles Larkyns commemorated by the following *affiche*, which our hero, on his return from his first morning chapel in the Michaelmas term, found in a conspicuous position on his oak:

COMMISSION SIGNED BY
THE VICE-CHANCELLOR OF
THE UNIVERSITY OF OXFORD.

MR. VERDANT GREEN to be an Oxford Undergraduate, *vice* Oxford Freshman, SOLD out.

It is generally found to be the case, that the youthful Undergraduate first seeks to prove he is no longer a 'Freshman,' by endeavouring to impose on the credulity of those young gentlemen who come up as Freshmen in his second term. And, in this, there is an analogy between the biped and the quadruped; for, the wild, gambolling, schoolboy elephant, when he has been brought into a new circle, and has been trained to new habits, will take pleasure in ensnaring and deluding his late companions in play.

The 'sells' by which our hero had been 'sold out' as a Freshman, now formed a stock in trade for the Undergraduate, which his experience enabled him to dispose of (with considerable interest) to the most credulous members of the generations of Freshmen who came up after him. Perhaps no Freshman had ever gone through a more severe course of hoaxing — to survive it — than Mr. Verdant Green; and yet, by a system of retaliation, only paralleled by the quadrupedal case of the before-mentioned elephant, and the biped-beadle case of the illustrious Mr. Bumble, who after having his own ears boxed by the late Mrs. Corney, relieved his feelings by boxing the ears of the small boy who opened the gate for him, — our hero took the greatest delight in seeking every opportunity to play off upon a Freshman some one of those numerous hoaxes which had been so successfully practised on himself. And while, in referring to the early part of his University career, he omitted all mention of such anecdotes as displayed his own personal credulity in the strongest light — which anecdotes the faithful historian has thought fit to record, — he, nevertheless, dwelt with extreme pleasure on the reminiscences of a few isolated facts, in which he himself appeared in the character of the hoaxer.

These facts, when neatly garnished with a little fiction, made very palatable dishes for University entertainment, and were served up by our hero, when he went 'down into the country,' to select parties of relatives and friends (N.B. — Females preferred). On such occasions, the following hoax formed Mr. Verdant Green's *piece de resistance*.

2

Mr. Verdant Green
Does as he has Been Done By

One morning, Mr. Verdant Green and Mr. Bouncer were lounging in the venerable gateway of Brazenface. The former gentleman, being of an amiable, tame-rabbit-keeping disposition, was making himself very happy by whistling popular airs to the Porter's pet bullfinch, who was laboriously engaged on a small tread-mill, winding up his private supply of water. Mr. Bouncer, being of a more volatile temperament, was amusing himself by asking the Porter's opinion on the foreign policy of Great Britain, and by making very audible remarks on the passers-by. His attention was at length riveted by the appearance on the other side of the street, of a modest-looking young gentleman, who appeared to be so ill at ease in his frock-coat and 'stick-up' collars, as to lead to the strong presumption that he wore those articles of manly dress for the first time.

'I'll bet you a bottle of blacking, Giglamps,' said little Mr. Bouncer, as he directed our hero's attention to the stranger, 'that this respected party is an intending Freshman. Look at his customary suits of solemn black, as Othello, or Hamlet, or some other swell, says in Shakespeare. And, besides his black go-to-meeting bags, please to observe,' continued the little gentleman, in the tone of a wax-work showman; 'please to *h*observe the pecooliarity hof the hair-chain, likewise the straps of the period. Look! he's coming this way. Giglamps, I vote we take a rise out of the youth. Hem! Good morning! Can we have the pleasure of assisting you in anything?'

'Yes, sir! thank you, sir,' replied the youthful stranger, who was flushing like a girl up to the very roots of his curly, auburn hair; 'perhaps, sir, you can direct me to Brazenface College, sir?'

'Well, sir! it's not at all improbable, sir, but what I could, sir;' replied Mr. Bouncer; 'but, perhaps, sir, you'll first favour me with your name, and your business there, sir.'

'Certainly, sir!' rejoined the stranger; and, while he fumbled at his card-case, the experienced Mr. Bouncer whispered to our hero, 'Told you he was a sucking Freshman, Giglamps! He has got a bran new card-case, and says 'sir' at the sight of the academicals.' The card handed to Mr. Bouncer, bore the name of 'MR. JAMES PUCKER;' and, in smaller characters in the corner of the card, were the words, '*Brazenface College, Oxford*.'

'I came, sir,' said the blushing Mr. Pucker, 'to enter for my matriculation examination, and I wished to see the gentleman who will have to examine me, sir.'

'The doose you do!' said Mr. Bouncer sternly; 'then young man, allow me to say, that you've regularly been and gone and done it, and put your foot in it most completely.'

'How-ow-ow, how, sir?' stammered the dupe.

'How?' replied Mr. Bouncer, still more sternly; 'do you mean to brazen out your offence by asking how? What *could* have induced you, sir, to have had printed on this card the name of this College, when you've not a prospect of belonging to it — it may be for years, it may be for never, as the bard says. You've committed a most grievous offence against the University statutes, young gentleman; and so this gentleman here — Mr. Pluckem, the junior examiner — will tell you!' and with that, little Mr. Bouncer nudged Mr. Verdant Green, who took his cue with astonishing aptitude, and glared through his glasses at the trembling Mr. Pucker, who stood blushing, and bowing, and heartily repenting that his school-boy vanity had led him to invest four-and-sixpence in '100 cards, and plate, engraved with name and address.'

'Put the cards in your pocket, sir, and don't let me see them again!' said our hero in his newly-confirmed title of the junior examiner; quite rejoiced at the opportunity afforded him of proving to his friend that *he* was no longer a Freshman.

'He forgives you for the sake of your family, young man!' said Mr. Bouncer with pathos; 'you've come to the right shop, for *this* is Brazenface; and you've come just at the right time, for here is the gentleman who will assist Mr. Pluckem in examining you;' and Mr. Bouncer pointed to Mr. Four-in-hand Fosbrooke, who was coming up the street on his way from the Schools, where he was making a very laudable (but as it proved, futile) endeavour 'to get through his smalls,' or, in other words, to pass his Little-go examination. The hoax which had been suggested to the ingenious mind of Mr. Bouncer, was based upon the fact of Mr. Fosbrooke's being properly got-up for his sacrifice in a white tie, and a pair of very small bands — the two articles, which, with the usual academicals, form the costume demanded by Alma Mater of all her children when they take their places in her Schools. And, as Mr. Fosbrooke was far too politic a gentleman to irritate the Examiners by appearing in a 'loud' or sporting costume, he had carried out the idea of clerical character suggested by the bands and choker, by a quiet, gentlemanly suit of black, which, he had fondly hoped, would have softened his Examiners' manners, and not permitted them to be brutal.

Mr. Four-in-hand Fosbrooke, therefore, to the unsophisticated eye of the blushing Mr. Pucker, presented a very fine specimen of the Examining Tutor; and this impression on Mr. Pucker's mind was heightened by Mr. Fosbrooke, after a few minutes' private conversation with the other two gentlemen, turning to him, and saying, 'It will be extremely inconvenient to me to examine you now; but as you probably wish to return home as soon as possible, I will endeavour to conclude the business at once — this gentleman, Mr. Pluckem,' pointing to our hero, 'having kindly promised to assist me. Mr. Bouncer, will you have the goodness to follow with the young gentleman to my rooms?'

Leaving Mr. Pucker to express his thanks for this great kindness, and Mr. Bouncer to plunge him into the depths of trepidation by telling him terrible *stories* of the Examiner's fondness for rejecting the candidates for examination, Mr. Fosbrooke and our hero ascended to the rooms of the former, where they hastily cleared away cigar-boxes and pipes, turned certain French pictures with their faces to the wall, and covered over with an outspread *Times* a regiment of porter and spirit bottles which had just been smuggled in, and were drawn up rank-and-file on the sofa. Having made this preparation, and furnished the table with pens, ink, and scribble-paper, Mr. Bouncer and the victim were admitted.

'Take a seat, sir,' said Mr. Fosbrooke, gravely; and Mr. Pucker put his hat on the ground, and sat down at the table in a state of blushing nervousness. 'Have you been at a public school?'

'Yes, sir,' stammered the victim; 'a very public one, sir; it was a boarding-school, sir; forty boarders, and thirty day-boys, sir; I was a day-boy, sir, and in the first class.'

'First class of an uncommon slow train!' muttered Mr. Bouncer.

'And are you going back to the boarding-school?' asked Mr. Verdant Green, with the air of an assistant judge.

'No sir,' replied Mr. Pucker, 'I have just done with it; quite done with school, sir, this last half; and papa is going to put me to read with a clergyman until it is time for me to come to college.'

'Refreshing innocence!' murmured Mr. Bouncer; while Mr. Fosbrooke and our hero conferred together, and hastily wrote on two sheets of the scribble-paper.

'Now, sir,' said Mr. Fosbrooke to the victim, after a paper had been completed, 'let us see what your Latin writing is like. Have the goodness to turn what I have written into Latin; and be very careful, sir,' added Mr. Fosbrooke, sternly, 'be very careful that it is Cicero's Latin, sir!' and he handed Mr. Pucker a sheet of paper, on which he had scribbled the following:

'TO BE TRANSLATED INTO PROSE-Y LATIN, IN THE MANNER OF CICERO'S ORATIONS AFTER DINNER.

'If, therefore, any on your bench, my luds, or in this assembly, should entertain an opinion that the proximate parts of a mellifluous mind are for ever conjoined and unconnected, I submit to you, my luds, that it will of necessity follow, that such clandestine conduct being a mere nothing, — or, in the noble language of our philosophers, bosh, — every individual act of overt misunderstanding will bring interminable limits to the empiricism of thought, and will rebound in the very lowest degree to the credit of the malefactor.'

‘TO BE TURNED INTO LATIN AFTER THE MANNER OF THE ANIMALS OF TACITUS.

> ‘She went into the garden to cut a cabbage to make an apple-pie. Just then, a great she-bear coming down the street, poked its nose into the shop-window. ‘What! no soap?’ So he died, and she (very imprudently) married the barber. And there were present at the wedding the Joblillies, and the Piccannies, and the Gobelites, and the great Panjandrum himself, with the little button on top. So they all set to playing Catch-who-catch-can, till the gunpowder ran out at the heels of their boots.’

It was well for the purposes of the hoaxers that Mr. Pucker’s trepidation prevented him from making a calm perusal of the paper; and he was nervously doing his best to turn the nonsensical English word by word into equally nonsensical Latin, when his limited powers of Latin writing were brought to a full stop by the untranslateable word ‘Bosh’. As he could make nothing of this, he wiped the perspiration from his forehead, and gazed appealingly at the benignant features of Mr. Verdant Green. The appealing gaze was answered by our hero ordering Mr. Pucker to hand in his paper for examination, and to endeavour to answer the questions which he and his brother examiner had been writing down for him.

Mr. Pucker took the two papers of questions, and read as follows:

'HISTORY.

'1. Draw a historical parallel (after the manner of Plutarch) between Hannibal and Annie Laurie.

'2. What internal evidence does the Odyssey afford, that Homer sold his Trojan war-ballads at three yards an obolus?

'3. Show the strong presumption there is, that Nox was the god of battles.

'4. State reasons for presuming that the practice of lithography may be traced back to the time of Perseus and the Gorgon's head.

'5. In what way were the shades on the banks of the Styx supplied with spirits?

'6. Show the probability of the College Hornpipe having been used by the students of the Academia; and give passages from Thucydides and Tennyson in support of your answer.

'7. Give a brief account of the Roman Emperors who visited the United States, and state what they did there.
'8. Show from the redundancy of the word {gas} in Sophocles, that gas must have been used by the Athenians; also state, if the expression {oi barbaroi} would seem to signify that they were close shavers.
'9. Show from the words 'Hoc erat in votis' (Sat. VI., Lib. II.,) that Horace's favourite wine was hock, and that he meant to say 'he always voted for hock.'
'10. Draw a parallel between the Children in the Wood and Achilles in the Styx.
'11. When it is stated that Ariadne, being deserted by Theseus, fell in love with Bacchus, is it the poetical way of asserting that she took to drinking to drown her grief?
'12. Name the *prima donnas* who have appeared in the operas of Virgil and Horace since the 'Virgilii Opera,' and 'Horatii Opera' were composed.'

'EUCLID, ARITHMETIC, and ALGEBRA.

'1. 'The extremities of a line are points.' Prove this by the rule of railways.

‘2. Show the fallacy of defining an angle, as ‘a worm at one end and a fool at the other.’

‘3. If one side of a triangle be produced, what is there to prevent the other two sides from also being brought forward?

‘4. Let A and B be squares having their respective boundaries in E and W ends, and let C and D be circles moving in them; the circle D will be superior to the circle C.

‘5. In equal circles, equal figures from various squares will stand upon the same footing.

‘6. If two parts of a circle fall out, the one part will cut the other.

‘7. Describe a square which shall be larger than Belgrave Square.

‘8. If the gnomon of a sun-dial be divided into two equal, and also into two unequal parts, what would be its value?

‘9. Describe a perpendicular triangle having the squares of the semi-circle equal to half the extremity between the points of section.

‘10. If an Austrian florin is worth 5.61 francs, what will be the value of Pennsylvanian bonds? Prove by rule-of-three inverse.

'11. If seven horses eat twenty-five acres of grass in three days, what will be their condition on the fourth day? Prove by practice.

'12. If a coach-wheel, 6 5/30 in diameter and 5 9/47 in circumference, makes 240 4/19 revolutions in a second, how many men will it take to do the same piece of work in ten days?

'13. Find the greatest common measure of a quart bottle of Oxford port.

'14. Find the value of a 'bob,' a 'tanner,' 'a joey,' and a 'tizzy.'

'15. Explain the common denominators 'brick,' 'trump,' 'spoon,' 'muff,' and state what was the greatest common denominator in the last term.

'16. Reduce two academical years to their lowest terms.

'17. Reduce a Christ Church tuft to the level of a Teddy Hall man.

'18. If a Freshman *A* have any mouth *x*, and a bottle of wine *y*, show how many applications of x to *y* will place *y+y* before *A*.'

Mr. Pucker did not know what to make of such extraordinary and unexpected questions. He blushed, attempted to write, fingered his curls, tried to collect his faculties, and then appeared to give himself over to despair; whereupon little Mr. Bouncer was seized with an immoderate fit of coughing which had well nigh brought the farce to its *denouement*.

'I'm afraid, young gentleman,' said Mr. Four-in-hand Fosbrooke, as he carelessly settled his white tie and bands, 'I am afraid, Mr. Pucker, that your learning is not yet up to the Brazenface standard. We are particularly cautious about admitting any gentleman whose acquirements are not of the highest order. But we will be as lenient to you as we are able, and give you one more chance to retrieve yourself. We will try a little *viva voce*, Mr. Pucker. Perhaps, sir, you will favour me with your opinions on the Fourth Punic War, and will also give me a slight sketch of the constitution of ancient Heliopolis.'

Mr. Pucker waxed, if possible, redder and hotter than before[,] he gasped like a fish out of water; and, like Dryden's prince, 'unable to conceal his pain,' he

'Sigh'd and look'd, sigh'd and look'd,
Sigh'd and look's, and sigh'd again.'

But all was to no purpose: he was unable to frame an answer to Mr. Fosbrooke's questions.

'Ah, sir,' continued his tormentor, 'I see that you will not do for us yet awhile, and I am therefore under the painful necessity of rejecting you. I should advise you, sir, to read hard for another twelvemonths, and endeavour to master those subjects in which you have now failed. For, a young man, Mr. Pucker, who knows nothing about the Fourth Punic War, and the constitution of ancient Heliopolis, is quite unfit to be enrolled among the members of such a learned college as Brazenface. Mr. Pluckem quite coincides with me in this decision.' (Here Mr. Verdant Green gave a Burleigh nod.) 'We feel very sorry for you, Mr. Pucker, and also for your unfortunate family; but we recommend you to add to your present stock of knowledge, and to keep those visiting-cards for another twelve-month.' And Mr. Fosbrooke and our hero — disregarding poor Mr. Pucker's entreaties that they would consider his pa and ma, and would please to matriculate him this once, and he would read very hard, indeed he would — turned to Mr. Bouncer and gave some private instructions, which caused that gentleman immediately to vanish, and seek out Mr. Robert Filcher.

Five minutes after, that excellent Scout met the dejected Mr. Pucker as he was crossing the Quad on his way from Mr. Fosbrooke's rooms.

'Beg your pardon, sir,' said Mr. Filcher, touching his forehead; for, as Mr. Filcher, after the manner of his tribe, never was seen in a head-covering, he was unable to raise his hat or cap; 'beg your pardon, sir! but was you a lookin' for the party as examines the young gents for their matrickylation?'

'Eh? — no! I have just come from him,' replied Mr. Pucker, dolefully.

'Beg your pardon, sir,' remarked Mr. Filcher, 'but his rooms ain't that way at all. Mr. Slowcoach, as is the party you *ought* to have seed, has *his* rooms quite in a hopposite direction, sir; and he's the honly party as examines the matrickylatin' gents.'

'But I *have* been examined,' observed Mr. Pucker, with the air of a plucked man; 'and I am sorry to say that I was rejected, and — '

'I dessay, sir,' interrupted Mr. Filcher; 'but I think it's a 'oax, sir!'

'A what?' stammered Mr. Pucker.

'A 'oax — a sell;' replied the Scout confidentially. 'You see, sir, I think some of the gents have been makin' a little game of you, sir; they often does with fresh parties like you, sir, that seem fresh and hinnocent like; and I dessay they've been makin' believe to examine you, sir, and a pretendin' that you wasn't clever enough. But they don't mean no harm, sir; it's only their play, bless you!'

'Then,' said Mr. Pucker, whose countenance had been gradually clearing with every word the Scout spoke; 'then I'm not really rejected, but have still a chance of passing my examination?'

'Percisely so, sir,' replied Mr. Filcher; 'and — hexcuse me, sir, for a hintin' of it to you, — but, if you would let me adwise you, sir, you wouldn't go for to mention anythin' about the 'oax to Mr. Slowcoach; *he* wouldn't be pleased, sir, and *you'd* only get laughed at. If you like to go to him now, sir, I know he's in his rooms, and I'll show you the way there with the greatest of pleasure.'

Mr. Pucker, immensely relieved in mind, gladly put himself under the Scout's guidance, and was admitted into the presence of Mr. Slowcoach. In twenty minutes after this he issued from the examining tutor's rooms with a joyful countenance, and again encountered Mr. Robert Filcher.

'Hope you've done the job this time, sir,' said the Scout.

'Yes,' replied the radiant Mr. Pucker; 'and at two o'clock I am to see the Vice-Chancellor; and I shall be able to come to college this time next year.'

'Werry glad of it, indeed, sir!' observed Mr.

Filcher, with genuine emotion, and an eye to future perquisites; 'and I suppose, sir, you didn't say a word about the 'oax?'

'Not a word!' replied Mr. Pucker.

'Then, sir,' said Mr. Filcher, with enthusiasm, 'hexcuse me, but you're a trump, sir! And Mr. Fosbrooke's compliments to you, sir, and he'll be 'appy if you'll come up into his rooms, and take a glass of wine after the fatigues of the examination. And, — hexcuse me again, sir, for a hintin' of it to you, but of course you can't be aweer of the customs of the place, unless somebody tells you on 'em, — I shall be werry glad to drink your werry good health, sir.'

Need it be stated that the blushing Mr. Pucker, delirious with joy at the sudden change in the state of affairs, and the delightful prospect of being a member of the University, not only tipped Mr. Filcher a five-shilling piece, but also paid a second visit to Mr. Fosbrooke's rooms, where he found that gentleman in his usual costume, and by him was introduced to the Mr. Pluckem, who now bore the name of Mr. Verdant Green? Need it be stated that the nervous Mr. Pucker blushed and laughed, and laughed and blushed, while his two pseudo-examiners took wine with him in the most friendly manner; Mr. Bouncer pronouncing him to be 'an out-and-outer, and no mistake!' And need it be stated that, after this undergraduate display of hoaxing, Mr. Verdant Green would feel exceedingly offended were he still to be called 'an Oxford Freshman?'

3

Mr. Verdant Green Endeavours to Keep his Spirits Up by Pouring Spirits Down

It was the evening of the fifth of November; the day which the Protestant youth of England dedicate to the memory of that martyr of gunpowder, the firework Faux, and which the youth of Oxford, by a three months' anticipation of the calendar, devote to the celebration of those scholastic sports for which the day of St. Scholastica the Virgin was once so famous.

Rumour with its hundred tongues had spread far and wide the news, that a more than ordinary demonstration would be made of the might of Town, and that this demonstration would be met by a corresponding increase of prowess on the side of Gown. It was darkly whispered that the purlieus of Jericho would send forth champions to the fight. It was mentioned that the Parish of St. Thomas would be powerfully represented by its Bargee lodgers. It was confidently reported that St. Aldate's would come forth in all its olden strength. It was told as a fact that St. Clement's had departed from the spirit of clemency, and was up in arms. From an early hour of the evening, the Townsmen had gathered in threatening groups; and their determined aspect, and words of chaff, had told of the coming storm. It was to be a tremendous Town and Gown!

The Poet has forcibly observed —

> 'Strange that there should such
> diff'rence be,
> 'Twixt Tweedledum and Tweedledee!'

But the difference between Town and Gown, is not to be classed with the Tweedledum and Tweedledee difference. It is something more than a mere difference of two letters. The lettered Gown lorded it over the unlettered Town: the plebeian Town was perpetually snubbed by the aristocratic Gown. If Gown even wished to associate with Town, he could only do so under certain restrictions imposed by the statutes; and Town was thus made to feel exceedingly honoured by the gracious condescension of Gown. But Town, moreover, maintained its existence, that it might contribute to the pleasure and amusements, the needs and necessities, of Gown. And very expensively was Town occasionally made to pay for its existence; so expensively indeed, that if it had not been for the great interest which Town assumed on Gown's account, the former's business-life would have soon failed. But, on many accounts, or rather, *in* many accounts, Gown was deeply indebted to Town; and, although Gown was often loth to own the obligation, yet Town never forgot it, but always placed it to Gown's credit. Occasionally, in his early freshness, Gown would seek to compensate Town for his obliging favours; but Town would gently run counter to this wish, and preferred that the evidences of Gown's friendly intercourse with him should accumulate, until he could, with renewed interest (as we understand from the authority of an aged pun), obtain his payments by Degrees.

When Gown was absent, Town was miserable: it was dull; it did nothing; it lost its customer-y application to business. When Gown returned, there was no small change, — the benefit was a sovereign one to Town. Notes, too, passed between them; of which, those received by Town were occasionally of intrinsic value. Town thanked Gown for these, — even thanked him when his civility had only been met by checks, — and smirked, and fawned, and flattered; and Gown patronised Town, and was offensively condescending. What a relief then must it have been to the pent-up feelings of Town, when the Saturnalia of a Guy-Faux day brought its usual license, and Town could stand up against Gown and try a game of fisticuffs! And if, when there was a cry 'To arms!' we could always settle the dispute in an English fashion with those arms with which we have been supplied by nature, there would then, perhaps, be fewer weeping widows and desolate orphans in the world than there are just at present.

On the evening of the fifth of November, then, Mr. Bouncer's rooms were occupied by a wine-party; and, among the gentlemen assembled, we noticed (as newspaper reporters say), Mr. Verdant Green, Mr. Charles Larkyns, Mr. Fosbrooke, Mr. Smalls, and Mr. Blades. The table was liberally supplied with wine; and a 'dessert at eighteen-pence per head,' — as Mr. Bouncer would afterwards be informed through the medium of his confectioner's bill; — and, while an animated conversation was being held on the expected Town and Gown, the party were fortifying themselves for the *emeute* by a rapid consumption of the liquids before them. Our hero, and some of the younger ones of the party, who had not yet left off their juvenile likings, were hard at work at the dessert in that delightful, disregardless-of-dyspepsia manner, in which boys so love to indulge, even when they have passed into University *men*. As usual, the *bouquet* of the wine was somewhat interfered with by those narcotic odours, which, to a smoker, are as the gales of Araby the Blest.

Mr. Blades was conspicuous among the party, not only from his dimensions, — or, as he phrased it, from 'his breadth of beam,' — but also from his free-and-easy costume. 'To get himself into wind,' as he alleged, Mr. Blades had just been knocking the wind out of the Honourable Flexible Shanks (youngest son of the Earl of Buttonhole), a Tuft from Christ Church, who had left his luxurious rooms in the Canterbury Quad chiefly for the purpose of preparing himself for the forthcoming Town and Gown, by putting on the gloves with his boating friend. The bout having terminated by Mr. Flexible Shanks having been sent backwards into a tray of wine-glasses with which Mr. Filcher was just entering the room, the gloves were put aside, and the combatants had an amicable set-to at a bottle of Carbonell's 'Forty-four,' which Mr. Bouncer brought out of a wine-closet in his bedroom for their especial delectation. Mr. Blades, who was of opinion that, in dress, ease should always be consulted before elegance, had not resumed that part of his attire of which he had divested himself for fistianic purposes; and, with a greater display of linen than is usually to be seen in society, was seated comfortably in a lounging chair, smoking the pipe of peace. Since he had achieved the proud feat of placing the Brazenface boat at the head of the river, Mr. Blades had gained increased renown, more especially in his own college, where he was regarded in the light of a tutelary river deity; and, as training was not going on, he was now enabled to indulge in a second glass of wine, and also in the luxury of a cigar. Mr. Blades' shirt-sleeves were turned up so as to display the anatomical proportion of his arms; and little Mr. Bouncer, with the grave aspect of a doctor feeling a pulse, was engaged in fingering his deltoid and biceps muscles, and in uttering panegyrics on his friend's torso-of-Hercules condition.

'My gum, Billy!' (it must be observed, *en passant*, that, although the name given to Mr. Blades at an early age was Frank, yet that when he was not called 'old Blades,' he was always addressed as 'Billy,' — it being a custom which has obtained in universities, that wrong names should be familiarly given to certain gentlemen, more as a mark of friendly intimacy than of derision or caprice.)

'My gum, Billy!' observed Mr. Bouncer, 'you're as hard as nails! What an extensive assortment of muscles you've got on hand, — to say nothing about the arms. I wish I'd got such a good stock in trade for our customers to-night; I'd soon sarve 'em out, and make 'em sing peccavi.'

'The fact is,' said Mr. Flexible Shanks, who was leaning smoking against the mantelpiece behind him, 'Billy is like a respectable family of bivalves — he is nothing but mussels.'

'Or like an old Turk,' joined in Mr. Bouncer, 'for he's a regular Mussulman.'

'Oh! Shanks! Bouncer!' cried Charles Larkyns, 'what stale jokes! Do open the window, somebody, — it's really offensive.'

'Ah!' said Mr. Blades, modestly, 'you only just wait till Footelights brings the Pet, and then you'll see real muscles.'

'It was rather a good move,' said Mr. Cheke, a gentleman Commoner of Corpus, who was lounging in an easy chair, smoking a meerschaum through an elastic tube a yard long, — 'it was rather a good move of yours, Fossy,' he said, addressing himself to Mr. Four-in-hand Fosbrooke, 'to secure the Pet's services. The feller will do us some service, and will astonish the *oi polloi* no end.'

'Oh! how prime it *will* be,' cried little Mr. Bouncer, in ecstacies with the prospect before him, 'to see the Pet pitching into the cads, and walking into their small affections with his one, two, three! And don't I just pity them when he gets them into Chancery! Were you ever in Chancery, Giglamps?'

'No, indeed!' replied the innocent Mr. Verdant Green; 'and I hope that I shall always keep out of it: lawsuits are 'so very disagreeable and expensive.'

Mr. Bouncer had only time to remark *sotto voce* to Mr. Flexible Shanks, 'it is so jolly refreshing to take a rise out of old Giglamps!' when a knock at the oak was heard; and, as Mr. Bouncer roared out, 'Come in!' the knocker entered. He was rather dressy in his style of costume, and wore his long dark hair parted in the middle. Opening the door, and striking into an attitude, he exclaimed in a theatrical tone and manner: 'Scene, Mr. Bouncer's rooms in Brazenface: in the centre a table, at which Mr. B. and party are discovered drinking log-juice, and smoking cabbage-leaves. Door, left, third entrance; enter the Putney Pet. Slow music; lights half-down.' And standing on one side, the speaker motioned to a second gentleman to enter the room.

There was no mistaking the profession of this gentleman; even the inexperience of Mr. Verdant Green did not require to be informed that the Putney Pet was a prizefighter. 'Bruiser' was plainly written in his personal appearance, from his hard-featured, low-browed, battered, hang-dog face, to his thickset frame, and the powerful muscular development of the upper part of his person. His close-cropped thatch of hair was brushed down tightly to his head, but was permitted to burst into the luxuriance of two small ringlets, which dangled in front of each huge ear, and were as carefully curled and oiled as though they had graced the face of beauty. The Pet was attired in a dark olive-green cutaway coat, buttoned over a waistcoat of a violent-coloured plaid, — a pair of white cord trousers that fitted tightly to the leg, — and a white-spotted blue handkerchief, which was twisted round a neck that might have served as a model for the Minotaur's. In his mouth, the Pet cherished, according to his wont, a sprig of parsley; small fragments of which herb he was accustomed to chew and spit out, as a pleasing relief to the monotony of conversation.

The Pet, after having been proclaimed victor in more than one of those playfully frolicsome 'Frolics of the Fancy,' in which nobly born but ignobly-minded 'Corinthians' formerly invested so much interest and money, had at length matched his powers against the gentleman who bore the title of 'the champion of the ring'; but, after a protracted contest of two hours and a half, in which one hundred and nineteen rounds had been fought, the Pet's eyes had been completely closed up by an amusing series of blows from the heavy fists of the more skilful champion; and as the Pet, moreover, was so battered and bruised, and was altogether so 'groggy' that he was barely able to stand up to be knocked down, his humane second had thrown up the sponge in acknowledgment of his defeat. But though unable to deprive the champion of his belt, yet — as *Tintinnabulum's Life* informed its readers on the following Sunday, in its report of this 'matchless encounter,' — the Putney Pet had 'established a reputation;' and a reputation *is* a reputation, even though it be one which may be offensive to the nostrils. Retiring, therefore, from the more active public duties of his profession, he took unto himself a wife and a beershop, — for it seems to be a freak of 'the Fancy,' when they retire from one public line to go into another, — and placing the former in charge of the latter, the Pet came forth to the world as a 'Professor of the noble art of Self-defence.'

It was in this phase of his existence, that Mr. Fosbrooke had the pleasure of forming his acquaintance. Mr. Fosbrooke had received a card, which intimated that the Pet would have great pleasure in giving him '*lessons in the noble and manly art of Self-defence, either at the gentleman's own residence, or at the Pet's spacious Sparring Academy, 5, Cribb Court, Drury Lane, which is fitted up with every regard to the comfort and convenience of his pupils. Gloves are provided. N.B. — Ratting sports at the above crib every evening. Plenty of rats always on hand. Use of the Pit gratis.*' Mr. Fosbrooke, having come to the wise conclusion that every Englishman ought to know how to be able to use his fists in case of need, and being quite of the opinion of the gentleman who said: — 'my son should even learn to box, for do we not meet with imposing toll-keepers, and insolent cabmen? and, as he can't call them out, he should be able to knock them down,' at once put himself under the Pet's tuition; and, as we have before seen, still kept up his practice with the gloves, when he had got to his own rooms at Brazenface.

But the Pet had other Oxford pupils than Mr. Fosbrooke; and he took such an affectionate interest in their welfare, that he came down from Town two or three times in each term, to see if his pupils' practice had made them perfect in the art. One of the Pet's pupils, was the gentleman who had now introduced him to Mr. Bouncer's rooms. His name was Foote, but he was commonly called 'Footelights;' the addition having been made to his name by way of *sobriquet* to express his unusual fondness for the stage, which amounted to so great a passion, that his very conversation was redolent of 'the footlights.' He had only been at St. John's a couple of terms, and Mr. Fosbrooke had picked up his acquaintance through the medium of the Pet, and had afterwards made him known to most of the men who were now assembled at Mr. Bouncer's wine.

'Your servant, gents!' said the Pet, touching his forehead, and making a scrape with his leg, by way of salutation.

'Hullo, Pet!' returned Mr. Bouncer; 'bring yourself to an anchor, my man.' The Pet accordingly anchored himself by dropping on to the edge of a chair, and placing his hat underneath it; while Huz and Buz smelt suspiciously round his legs, and looked at him with an expression of countenance which bore a wonderful resemblance to that which they gazed upon.

'Never mind the dogs; they're amiable little beggars,' observed Mr. Bouncer, 'and they never bite any one except in play. Now then, Pet, what sort of liquors are you given to?

Here are Claret liquors, Port liquors, Sherry liquors, egg-flip liquors, Cup liquors. You pays your money, and you takes your choice!'

'Well, sir, thankee!' replied the Pet, 'I ain't no ways pertikler, but if you *have* sich a thing as a glass o' sperrits, I'd prefer that — if not objectionable.'

'In course not, Pet! always call for what you like. We keep all sorts of liquors, and are allowed to get drunk on the premises. Ain't we, Giglamps?' Firing this raking shot as he passed our hero, little Mr. Bouncer dived into the cupboard which served as his wine-bin, and brought therefrom two bottles of brandy and whiskey which he set before the Pet. 'If you like gin or rum, or cherry-brandy, or old old-tom, better than these liquors,' said Mr. Bouncer, astonishing the Pet with the resources of a College wine-cellar, 'just say the word, and you shall have them. 'I can call spirits from the vasty deep;' as Shikspur says. How will you take it, Pet? Neat, or adulterated? Are you for *callidum cum*, or *frigidum sine* — for hot-with, or cold-without?'

'I generally takes my sperrits 'ot, sir — if not objectionable,' replied the Pet deferentially. Whereupon Mr. Bouncer seizing his speaking-trumpet, roared through it from the top of the stairs, 'Rob-ert! Rob-ert!' But, as

Mr. Filcher did not answer the summons, Mr. Bouncer threw up the window of his room, and bellowed out 'Rob-ert' in tones which must have been perfectly audible in the High Street. 'Doose take the feller, he's always over at the Buttery,' said the incensed gentleman.

'I'll go up to old Sloe's room, and get his kettle,' said Mr. Smalls; 'he teas all day long to keep himself awake for reading. If he don't mind, he'll blow himself up with his gunpowder tea before he can take his double-first.'

By the time Mr. Smalls had re-appeared with the kettle, Mr. Filcher had thought it prudent to answer his master's summons.

'Did you call, sir?' asked the scout, as though he was doubtful on that point.

'Call!' said Mr. Bouncer, with great irony; 'oh, no! of course not! I should rather think not! Do you suppose that you are kept here that parties may have the chance of hollering out their lungs for you? Don't answer me, sir! but get some hot water, and some more glasses; and be quick about it.' Mr. Filcher was gone immediately; and, in three minutes, everything was settled to Mr. Bouncer's satisfaction, and he gave Mr. Filcher farther orders to bring up coffee and anchovy toast, at half-past eight o'clock.

'Now, Pet, my beauty!' said the little gentleman, 'you just walk into the liquors; because you've got some toughish work before you, you know.'

The Pet did not require any pressing, but did as he was told; and, bestowing a collective nod on the company, drank their healths with the prefatory remark, 'I looks to-*wards* you gents!'

'Will you poke a smipe, Pet?' asked Mr. Bouncer, rather enigmatically; but, as he at the same time placed before Pet a 'yard of clay' and a box of cigars, the professor of the art of self-defence perceived that he was asked to smoke a pipe.

'That's right, Pet!' said the Honourable Flexible Shanks, condescendingly, as the prizefighter scientifically filled the bowl of his pipe; 'I'm glad to see you join us in a bit of smoke. We're all *Baccy*-nalians now!'

'Shanks, you're incorrigible!' said Charles Larkyns; 'and don't you remember what the *Oxford Parodies* say?' and in his clear, rich voice, Mr. Larkyns sang the two following verses to the air of 'Love not:' —

Smoke not, smoke not, your weeds nor
 pipes of clay;
Cigars they are made from leaves of
 cauliflowers;

Things that are soomed no duty e'er to
pay;
Grown, made, and smoked in a few
short hours.
Smoke not — smoke not!

Smoke not, smoke not, the weed you
smoke ma change
The healthfulness of your stomachic
tone;
Things to the eye grown queer and
passing strange;
All thoughts seem undefined — save
one — to be alone!
Smoke not — smoke not!

'I know what you're thinking about, Giglamps,' said Mr. Bouncer, as Charles Larkyns ceased his parody amid an approving clatter of glasses; 'you were thinking of your first weed on the night of Smalls' quiet party: wer'nt you now, old feller? Ah, you've learnt to poke a smipe, beautiful, since then. Pet, here's your health. I'll give you a toast and s*in*timent, gentlemen. May the Gown give the Town a jolly good hiding!' The sentiment was received with great applause, and the toast was drunk with all the honours, and followed by the customary but inappropriate chorus, 'For he's a jolly good fellow!' without the singing of which Mr. Bouncer could not allow any toast to pass.

'How many cads could you lick at once, one off and the other on?' asked Mr. Fosbrooke of the Pet, with the air of Boswell when he wanted to draw out the Doctor.

'Well, sir,' said the Pet, with the modesty of true genius, 'I wouldn't be pertickler to a score or so, as long as I'd got my back well up agin some'ut, and could hit out.'

'What an effective tableau it would be!' observed Mr. Foote, who had always an eye to dramatic situations. 'Enter the Pet, followed by twenty townspeople. First T.P. — Yield, traitor! Pet — Never! the man who would yield when ordered to do so, is unworthy the name of a Pet and an Englishman! Floors the twenty T.P.'s one after the other. Tableau, blue fire. Why, it would surpass the British sailor's broadsword combat for six, and bring down the house.'

'Talking of bringing down', said Mr. Blades, 'did you remember to bring down a cap and gown for the Pet, as I told you?'

'Well, I believe those *were* the stage directions,' answered Mr. Foote; 'but, really, the wardrobe was so ill provided that it would only supply a cap. But perhaps that will do for a super.'

'If by a super you mean a supernumerary, Footelights,' said Mr. Cheke, the gentleman

Commoner of Corpus, 'then the Pet isn't one. He's the leading character of what you would call the *dramatis personae*.'

'True,' replied Mr. Foote, 'he's cast for the hero; though he will create a new *role* as the walking-into-them gentleman.'

'You see, Footelights,' said Mr. Blades, 'that the Pet is to lead our forces; and we depend upon him to help us on to victory: and we must put him into academicals, not only because the town cads must think he is one of us, but also because the proctors might otherwise deprive us of his services — and old Towzer, the Senior Proctor, in particular, is sure to be all alive. Who's got an old gown?'

'I will lend mine with pleasure,' said Mr. Verdant Green.

'But you'll want it yourself,' said Mr. Blades.

'Why, thank you,' faltered our hero, 'I'd rather, I think, keep within college. I can see the — the fun — yes, the fun — from the window.'

'Oh, blow it, Giglamps!' ejaculated Mr. Bouncer, 'you'll never go to do the mean, and show the white feather, will you?'

'Music expressive of trepidation,' murmured Mr. Foote, by way of parenthesis.

'But,' pursued our hero, apologetically, 'there will be, I dare say, a large crowd.'

'A very powerful *caste*[sic], no doubt,' observed Mr. Foote.

'And I may get my — yes, my spectacles broken; and then' —

'And then, Giglamps,' said Mr. Bouncer, 'why, and then you shall be presented with another pair as a testimonial of affection from yours truly. Come, Giglamps, don't do the mean! a man of your standing, and with a chest like that!' and the little gentleman sounded on our hero's shirt-front, as doctors do when they stethoscope a patient. 'Come, Giglamps, old feller, you mustn't refuse. You didn't ought to was, as Shakespeare says.'

'Pardon me! Not Shakespeare, but Wright, in the 'Green Bushes,'' interrupted Mr. Foote, who was as painfully anxious as Mr. Payne Collier himself that the text of the great poet should be free from corruptions.

So Mr. Verdant Green, reluctantly, it must be confessed, suffered himself to be persuaded to join that section of the Gown which was to be placed under the leadership of the redoubted Pet; while little Mr. Bouncer, who had gone up into Mr. Sloe's rooms, and had vainly endeavoured to persuade that gentleman to join in the forthcoming *melee*, returned with an undergraduate's gown, and forthwith invested the Pet with it.

'I don't mind this 'ere mortar-board, sir,' remarked the professor of the noble art of self-defence, as he pointed to the academical cap which surmounted his head, 'I don't mind the mortar-board, sir; but I shall never be able to do nothink with this 'ere toggery on my shudders. I couldn't use my mawleys no how!' And the Pet illustrated his remark in a professional manner, by sparring at an imaginary opponent in a feeble and unscientific fashion.

'But you can tie the tail-curtain round your shoulders — like this!' said Mr. Fosbrooke, as he twisted his own gown tightly round him.

But the Pet had taken a decided objection to the drapery: 'The costume would interfere with the action,' as Mr. Foote remarked, 'and the management of a train requires great practice.'

'You see, sir,' said the Pet, 'I ain't used to the feel of it, and I couldn't go to business properly, or give a straight nosender no how. But the mortar-board ain't of so much consekvence.' So a compromise was made; and it was agreed that the Pet was to wear the academicals until he had arrived at the scene of action, where he could then pocket the gown, and resume it on any alarm of the Proctor's approach.

'Here, Giglamps, old feller! get a priming

of fighting-powder!' said little Mr. Bouncer to our hero, as the party were on the point of sallying forth; 'it'll make you hit out from your shoulder like a steam-engine with the chill off.' And, as Mr. Bouncer whispered to Charles Larkyns,

'So he kept his spirits up
By pouring spirits down,'

Verdant — who felt extremely nervous, either from excitement or from fear, or from a pleasing mixture of both sensations — drank off a deep draught of something which was evidently not drawn from Nature's spring or the college pump; for it first took away his breath, and made his eyes water; and it next made him cough, and endeavour to choke himself; and it then made his face flush, and caused him to declare that 'the first snob who 'sulted him should have a sound whopping'.

'Brayvo, Giglamps!' cried little Mr. Bouncer, as he patted him on the shoulder; 'come along! You're the right sort of fellow for a Town and Gown, after all!'

4

Mr. Verdant Green Discovers the Difference Between Town and Gown

It was ten minutes past nine, and Tom, with a sonorous voice, was ordering all College gates to be shut, when the wine party, which had just left Mr. Bouncer's room, passed round the corner of St. Mary's, and dashed across the High. The Town and Gown had already begun.

As usual, the Town had taken the initiative; and, in a dense body, had made their customary sweep of the High Street, driving all before them. After this gallant exploit had been accomplished to the entire satisfaction of the oppidans, the Town had separated into two or three portions, which had betaken themselves to the most probable fighting points, and had gone where glory waited them, thirsting for the blood, or, at any rate, for the bloody noses of the gowned aristocrats. Woe betide the luckless gownsman, who, on such an occasion, ventures abroad without an escort, or trusts to his own unassisted powers to defend himself! He is forthwith pounced upon by some score of valiant Townsmen, who are on the watch for these favourable opportunities for a display of their personal prowess, and he may consider himself very fortunate if he is able to get back to his College with nothing worse than black eyes and bruises. It is so seldom that the members of the Oxford snobocracy have the privilege afforded them of using their fists on the faces and persons of the members of the Oxford aristocracy, that when they *do* get the chance, they are unwilling to let it slip through their fingers. Dark tales have, indeed, been told, of solitary and unoffending undergraduates having, on such occasions, not only received a severe handling from those same fingers, but also having been afterwards, through their agency, bound by their own leading strings to the rails of the Radcliffe, and there left ignominiously to struggle, and shout for assistance. And darker tales still have been told of luckless Gownsmen having been borne 'leg and wing' fashion to the very banks of the Isis, and there ducked, amidst the jeers and taunts of their persecutors. But such tales as these are of too dreadful a nature for the conversation of Gownsmen, and are very properly believed to be myths scandalously propagated by the Town.

The crescent moon shone down on Mr. Bouncer's party, and gave ample light

To light *them* on *their* prey.

A noise and shouting, — which quickly made our hero's Bob-Acreish resolutions ooze out at his fingers' ends, — was heard coming from the direction of Oriel Street; and a small knot of Gownsmen, who had been cut off from a larger body, appeared, manfully retreating with their faces to the foe, fighting as they fell back, but driven by superior numbers up the narrow street, by St. Mary's Hall, and past the side of Spiers's shop into the High Street.

'Gown to the rescue!' shouted Mr. Blades as he dashed across the street; 'come on, Pet! here we are in the thick of it, just in the nick of time!' and, closely followed by Charles Larkyns, Mr. Fosbrooke, Mr. Smalls, Mr. Bouncer, Mr. Flexible Shanks, Mr. Cheke, Mr. Foote, and our hero, and the rest of the party, they soon plunged *in medias res*.

The movement was particularly well-timed, for the small body of Gownsmen were beginning to get roughly handled; but the succour afforded by the Pet and his party soon changed the aspect of affairs; and, after a brief skirmish, there was a temporary cessation of hostilities. As reinforcements poured in on either side, the mob which represented the Town, wavered, and spread themselves across on each side of the High; while a huge, lumbering bargeman, who appeared to be the generalissimo of their forces, delivered himself of a brief but energetic speech, in which he delivered his opinion of Gownsmen in general, and his immediate foes in particular, in a way which would have to be expressed in proper print chiefly by blanks, and which would have assuredly entailed upon him a succession of five-shilling fines, had he been in a court of justice, and before a magistrate.

'Here's a pretty blank, I don't think!' he observed in conclusion, as he pointed to Mr. Verdant Green, who was nervously settling his spectacles, and wishing himself safe back in his own rooms; 'I wouldn't give a blank for such a blank blank. I'm blank if he don't look as though he'd swaller'd a blank codfish, and had bust out into blank barnacles!' As the Bargee was apparently regarded by his party as a gentleman of infinite humour, his highly-flavoured blank remarks were received by them with shouts of laughter; while our hero obtained far more of the *digito monstrari* share of public notice than he wished for.

For some brief space, the warfare between the rival parties of Town and Gown continued to be one merely of words — a mutual discharge of *epea pteroenta* (*vulgariter* 'chaff'), in which a small amount of sarcasm was mingled with a large share of vituperation. At length, a slang rhyme of peculiar offensiveness was used to a Wadham gentleman, which so exasperated him that he immediately, by way of a forcible reply, sent his fist full into the speaker's face. On this, a collision took place between those who formed the outside of the crowd; and the Gowns flocked together to charge *en masse*. Mr. Verdant Green was not quite aware of this sudden movement, and, for a moment, was cut off from the rest.

This did not escape the eyes of the valiant Bargee, who had already singled out our hero as the one whom he could most easily punish, with the least chance of getting quick returns for his small profits. Forthwith, therefore, he rushed to his victim, and aimed a heavy blow at him, which Verdant only half avoided by stooping. Instinctively doubling his fists, our hero found that Necessity was, indeed, the mother of Invention; and, with a passing thought of what would be his mother's and Aunt Virginia's feelings could they see him fighting in the public streets with a common bargeman, he contrived to guard off the second blow. But at the next furious [lunge] of the Bargee he was not quite so fortunate, and, receiving that gentleman's heavy fist full in his forehead, he staggered backwards, and was only prevented from measuring his length on the pavement by falling against the iron gates of St. Mary's. The delighted Bargee was just on the point of putting the *coup de grace* to his attack, when, to Verdant's inexpressible delight and relief, his lumbering antagonist was sent sprawling by a well-directed blow on his right ear. Charles Larkyns, who had kept a friendly eye on our hero, had spied his condition, and had sprung to his assistance. He was closely followed by the Pet, who had divested himself of the gown which had encumbered his shoulders, and was now freely striking out in all directions. The fight had become general, and fresh combatants had sprung up on either side.

'Keep close to me, Verdant,' said Charles Larkyns, — quite unnecessarily, by the way, as our hero had no intention of doing otherwise until he saw a way to escape; 'keep close to me, and I'll take care you are not hurt.'

'Here ye are!' cried the Pet, as he set his back against the stone-work flanking the iron gates of the church, immediately in front of one of the curiously twisted pillars of the Porch; 'come on, half a dozen of ye, and let me have a rap at your smellers!' and he looked at the mob in the 'Come one, come all defiant' fashion of Fitz-James; while Charles Larkyns and Verdant set their backs against the church gates, and prepared for a rush.

The Bargee came up furious, and hit out wildly at Charles Larkyns; but science was more than a match for brute force; and, after receiving two or three blows which caused him to shake his head in a don't-like-it sort of way, he endeavoured to turn his attention to Mr. Verdant Green, who, with head in air, was taking the greatest care of his spectacles, and endeavouring to ward off the indiscriminate lunges of half a dozen townsmen. The Bargee's charitable designs on our hero were, however, frustrated by the opportune appearance of Mr. Blades and Mr. Cheke, the gentleman-commoner of Corpus, who, in their turn, were closely followed by Mr. Smalls and Mr. Flexible Shanks; and Mr. Blades exclaiming, 'There's a smasher for your ivories, my fine fellow!' followed up his remark with a practical application of his fist to the part referred to; whereupon the Bargee fell back with a howl, and gave vent to several curse-ory observations, and blank remarks.

All this time the Pet was laying about him in the most determined manner; and, to judge from his professional observations, his scientific acquirements were in full play. He had agreeable remarks for each of his opponents; and, doubtless, the punishment which they received from his stalwart arms came with more stinging force when the parts affected were pointed out by his illustrative language. To one gentleman he would pleasantly observe, as he tapped him on the chest, 'Bellows to mend for you, my buck!' or else, 'There's a regular rib-roaster for you!' or else, in the still more elegant imagery of the Ring, 'There's a squelcher in the breadbasket, that'll stop *your* dancing, my kivey!' While to another he would cheerfully remark, 'Your head-rails were loosened there, wasn't they?' or, 'How about the kissing-trap?' or, 'That draws the bung from the beer-barrel I'm a thinkin'.' While to another he would say, as a fact not to be disputed, 'You napp'd it heavily on your whisker-bed, didn't you?' or, 'That'll raise a tidy mouse on your ogle, my lad!' or, 'That'll take the bark from your nozzle, and distil the Dutch pink for you, won't it?' While to another he would mention as an interesting item of news, 'Now we'll tap your best October!' or, 'There's a crack on your snuff-box!' or, 'That'll damage your potato-trap!' Or else he would kindly inquire of one gentleman, 'What d'ye ask a pint for your cochineal dye?' or would amiably recommend another that, as his peepers were a goin' fast, he'd best put up the shutters, because the early-closing movement ought to be follered out. All this was done in the cheeriest manner; while, at the same time, the Pet proved himself to be not only a perfect master of his profession, but also a skilful adept in those figures of speech, or 'nice derangements of epitaphs,' as Mrs. Malaprop calls them, in which the admirers of the fistic art so much delight. At every blow, a fresh opponent either fell or staggered off; the supremacy of the Pet was complete, and his claim to be considered a Professor of the noble and manly art of Self-defence was triumphantly established. 'The Putney Pet' was a decidedly valuable acquisition to the side of Gown.

Soon the crowd became thinner, as those of the Town who liked to give, but not to receive hard blows, stole off to other quarters; and the Pet and his party would have been left peaceably to themselves. But this was not what they wanted, as long as fighting was going on elsewhere; even Mr. Verdant Green began to feel desperately courageous as the

Town took to their heels, and fled; and, having performed prodigies of valour in almost knocking down a small cad who had had the temerity to attack him, our hero felt himself to be a hero indeed, and announced his intention of pursuing the mob, and sticking close to Charles Larkyns, — taking especial care to do the latter.

'All the savage soul of *fight* was up';

and the Gown following the scattered remnant of the flying Town, ran them round by All Saints' Church, and up the Turl. Here another Town and Gown party had fought their way from the Corn-market; and the Gown, getting considerably the worst of the conflict, had taken refuge within Exeter College by the express order of the Senior Proctor, the Rev. Thomas Tozer, more familiarly known as 'old Towzer.' He had endeavoured to assert his proctorial authority over the mob of the townspeople; but the *profanum vulgus* had not only scoffed and jeered him, but had even torn his gown, and treated his velvet sleeves with the indignity of mud; while the only fireworks which had been exhibited on that evening had been let off in his very face. Pushed on, and hustled by the mob, and only partially protected by his Marshal and Bull-dogs, he was saved from further indignity by the arrival of a small knot of Gownsmen, who rushed to his rescue. Their number was too small, however, to make head against the mob, and the best that they could do was to cover the Proctor's retreat. Now, the Rev. Thomas Tozer was short, and inclined to corpulence, and, although not wanting for courage, yet the exertion of defending himself from a superior force, was not only a fruitless one, but was, moreover, productive of much unpleasantness and perspiration. Deeming, therefore, that discretion was the better part of valour, he fled (like those who tended, or *ought* to have attended to, the flocks of Mr. Norval, Sen.)

'for safety and for succour;'

and, being rather short of the necessary article of wind, by the time that he had reached Exeter College, he had barely breath enough left to tell the porter to keep the gate shut until he had assembled a body of Gownsmen to assist him in capturing those daring ringleaders of the mob who had set his authority at defiance. This was soon done; the call to arms was made, and every Exeter man who was not already out, ran to 'old Towzer's' assistance.

'Now, Porter,' said Mr. Tozer, 'unbar the gate without noise, and I will look forth to observe the position of the mob. Gentlemen, hold yourselves in readiness to secure the ringleaders.'

The porter undid the wicket, and the Rev. Thomas Tozer cautiously put forth his head. It was a rash act; for, no sooner had his nose appeared round the edge of the wicket, than it received a flattening blow from the fist of an active gentleman who, like a clever cricketer, had been on the lookout for an opportunity to get in to his adversary's wicket.

'Oh, this is painful! this is very painful!' ejaculated Mr. Tozer, as he rapidly drew in his head. 'Close the wicket directly, porter, and keep it fast.' It was like closing the gates of Hougomont. The active gentleman who had damaged Mr. Tozer's nose threw himself against the wicket, his comrades assisted him, and the porter had some difficulty in obeying the Proctor's orders.

'Oh, this is painful!' murmured the Rev. Thomas Tozer, as he applied a handkerchief to his bleeding nose; 'this is painful, this is very painful! this is exceedingly painful, gentlemen!'

He was immediately surrounded by sympathizing undergraduates, who begged him to allow them at once to charge the Town; but 'old Towzer's' spirit seemed to have been aroused by the indignity to which he had been forced so publicly to submit, and he replied that, as soon as the bleeding had ceased, he would lead them forth in person. An encouraging cheer followed this courageous resolve, and was echoed from without by the derisive applause of the Town.

When Mr. Tozer's nose had ceased to bleed, the signal was given for the gates to be thrown open; and out rushed Proctor, Marshal, Bull-dogs, and undergraduates. The Town was in great force, and the fight became desperate. To the credit of the Town, be it said, they discarded bludgeons and stones, and fought, in John Bull fashion, with their fists. Scarcely a stick was to be seen. Singling out his man, Mr. Tozer made at him valiantly, supported by his Bull-dogs, and a small band of Gownsmen. But the heavy gown and velvet sleeves were a grievous hindrance to the Proctor's prowess; and, although supported on either side by his two attendant Bull-dogs, yet the weight of his robes made poor Mr. Tozer almost as harmless as the blind King of Bohemia between his two faithful knights at the battle of Crecy; and, as each of the party had to look to, and fight for himself, the Senior

Proctor soon found himself in an awkward predicament.

The cry of 'Gown to the rescue!' therefore, fell pleasantly on his ears; and the reinforcement headed by Mr. Charles Larkyns and his party, materially improved the aspect of affairs on the side of Gown. Knocking down a cowardly fellow, who was using his heavy-heeled boots on the body of a prostrate undergraduate, Mr. Blades, closely followed by the Pet, dashed in to the Proctor's assistance; and never in a Town and Gown was assistance more timely rendered; for the Rev. Thomas Tozer had just received his first knock-down blow! By the help of Mr. Blades the fallen chieftain was quickly replaced upon his legs; while the Pet stepped before him, and struck out skilfully right and left. Ten more minutes of scientific pugilism, and the fate of the battle was decided. The Town fled every way; some round the corner by Lincoln College; some up the Turl towards Trinity; some down Ship Street; and some down by Jesus College, and Market Street. A few of the more resolute made a stand in Broad Street; but it was of no avail; and they received a sound punishment at the hands of the Gown, on the spot, where, some three centuries before, certain mitred Gownsmen had bravely suffered martyrdom.

Now, the Rev. Thomas Tozer was a strict disciplinarian, and, although he had so materially benefited by the Pet's assistance, yet, when he perceived that that pugilistic gentleman was not possessed of the full complement of academical attire, the duties of the Proctor rose superior to the gratitude of the Man; and, with all the sternness of an ancient Roman Father, he said to the Pet, 'Why have you not on your gown, sir?'

'I ax your pardon, guv'nor!' replied the Pet, deferentially; 'I didn't so much care about the mortar-board, but I couldn't do nothin' nohow with t'other thing, so I pocketted him; but some cove must have gone and prigged him, for he ain't here.'

'I am unable to comprehend the nature of your language, sir,' observed the Rev. Thomas Tozer, angrily; for, what with his own excitement, and the shades of evening which had stolen over and obscured the Pet's features, he was unable to read that gentleman's character and profession in his face, and therefore came to the conclusion that he was being chaffed by some impudent undergraduate. 'I don't in the least understand you, sir; but I desire at once to know your name, and College, sir!'

The Putney Pet stared. If the Rev. Thomas Tozer had asked him for the name of his

Academy, he would have been able to have referred him to his spacious and convenient Sparring Academy, 5, Cribb Court, Drury Lane; but the inquiry for his 'College,' was, in the language of his profession, a 'regular floorer'.

Mr. Blades, however, stepped forward, and explained matters to the Proctor, in a satisfactory manner.

'Well, well!' said the pacified Mr. Tozer to the Pet; 'you have used your skill very much to our advantage, and displayed pugilistic powers not unworthy of the athletes, and xystics of the noblest days of Rome. As a palaestrite you would have gained palms in the gymnastic exercises of the Circus Maximus. You might even have proved a formidable rival to Dares, who, as you, Mr. Blades, will remember, caused the death of Butes at Hector's tomb. You will remember, Mr. Blades, that Virgil makes mention of his 'humeros latos,' and says: —

> 'Nec quisquam ex agmine tanto
> Audet adire virum, manibusque
> inducere caestus;'

which, in our English idiom, would signify, that every one was afraid to put on the gloves with him. And, as your skill,' resumed Mr.

Tozer, turning to the Pet, 'has been exercised in defence of my person, and in upholding the authority of the University, I will overlook your offence in assuming that portion of the academical attire, to which you gave the offensive epithet of 'mortar-board'; more especially, as you acted at the suggestion and bidding of those who ought to have known better. And now, go home, sir, and resume your customary head-dress; and — stay! here's five shillings for you.'

'I'm much obleeged to you, guv'nor,' said the Pet, who had been listening with considerable surprise to the Proctor's quotations and comparisons, and wondering whether the gentleman named Dares, who caused the death of beauties, was a member of the P.R., and whether they made it out a case of manslaughter against him? and if the gaining palms in a circus was the customary 'flapper-shaking' before 'toeing the scratch for business?' — 'I'm much obleeged to you, guv'nor,' said the Pet, as he made a scrape with his leg; 'and, whenever you *does* come up to London, I 'ope you'll drop in at Cribb Court, and have a turn with the gloves!' And the Pet, very politely, handed one of his professional cards to the Rev. Thomas Tozer.

A little later than this, a very jovial supper party might have been seen assembled in a principal room at 'the Roebuck.' To enable them to be back within their college walls, and save their gates, before the hour of midnight should arrive, the work of consuming the grilled bones and welch-rabbits was going on with all reasonable speed, the heavier articles being washed down by draughts of 'heavy.' After the cloth was withdrawn, several songs of a miscellaneous character were sung by 'the professional gentlemen present,' including, 'by particular request,' the celebrated 'Marble Halls' song of our hero, which was given with more coherency than on a previous occasion, but was no less energetically led in its 'you-loved-me-still-the-same' chorus by Mr. Bouncer. The Pet was proudly placed on the right hand of the chairman, Mr. Blades; and, when his health was proposed, 'with many thanks to him for the gallant and plucky manner in which he had led on the Gown to a glorious victory,' the 'three times three,' and the 'one cheer more,' and the 'again,' and 'again,' and the 'one other little un!' were uproariously given (as Mr. Foote expressed it), 'by the whole strength of the company, assisted by Messrs. Larkyns, Smalls, Fosbrooke, Flexible Shanks, Cheke, and Verdant Green.'

The forehead of the last-named gentleman was decorated with a patch of brown paper, from which arose an aroma, as though of vinegar. The battle of 'Town and Gown' was over; and Mr. Verdant Green was among the number of the wounded.

5

Mr. Verdant Green is Favoured with Mr. Bouncer's Opinions Regarding an Undergraduate's Epistolary Communications to his Maternal Relative

'Come in, whoever you are! don't mind the dogs!' shouted little Mr. Bouncer, as he lay, in an extremely inelegant attitude, in a red morocco chair, which was considerably the worse for wear, chiefly on account of the ill-usage it had to put up with, in being made to represent its owner's antagonist, whenever Mr. Bouncer thought fit to practise his fencing.

'Oh! it's you and Giglamps is it, Charley? I'm just refreshing myself with a weed, for I've been desperately hard at work.'

'What! Harry Bouncer devoting himself to study! But this is the age of wonders,' said Charles Larkyns, who entered the room in company with Mr. Verdant Green, whose forehead still betrayed the effects of the blow he had received a few nights before.

'It ain't reading that I meant,' replied Mr.

Bouncer, 'though that always *does* floor me, and no mistake! and what's the use of their making us peg away so at Latin and Greek, I can't make out. When I go out into society, I don't want to talk about those old Greek and Latin birds that they make us get up. I don't want to ask any old dowager I happen to fall in with at a tea-fight, whether she believes all the crammers that Herodotus tells us, or whether she's well up in the naughty tales and rummy nuisances that we have to pass no end of our years in getting by heart. And when I go to a ball, and do the light fantastic, I don't want to ask my partner what she thinks about Euripides, or whether she prefers Ovid's Metamorphoses to Ovid's Art of Love, and all that sort of thing; and as for requesting her to do me a problem of Euclid, instead of working me any glorified slippers or woolleries, I'd scorn the *h*action. I ain't like you, Charley, and I'm not *guv* in the classics: I saw too much of the beggars while I was at Eton to take kindly to 'em; and just let me once get through my Greats, and see if I don't precious soon drop the acquaintance of those old classical parties!'

'No you won't, old fellow!' said Charles Larkyns; 'you'll find that they'll stick to you through life, just like poor relations, and you won't be able to shake them off. And you ought not to wish to do so, more especially as, in the end, you will find them to have been very rich relations.'

'A sort of 'O my prophetic soul, my uncle!' I suppose, Master Charley,' observed Mr. Bouncer; 'but what I meant when I said that I had been hard at work was, that I had been writing a letter; and, though I say it that ought not to say it, I flatter myself it's no end of a good letter.'

'Is it a love-letter?' asked Charles Larkyns, who was leaning against the mantelpiece, amusing himself with a cigar which he had taken from Mr. Bouncer's box.

'A love-letter?' replied the little gentleman, contemptuously — 'my gum! no; I should raything think not! I may have done many foolish things in my life, but I can't have the tender passion laid to my charge. No! I've been writing my letter to the Mum: I always write to her once a term.' Mr. Bouncer, it must be observed, always referred to his maternal relative (his father had been long dead) by the epithet of 'the Mum.'

'Once a term!' said our hero, in a tone of surprise; 'why I always write home once or twice every week.'

'You don't mean to say so, Giglamps!' replied Mr. Bouncer, with admiration. 'Well, some fellers have what you call a genius for that sort of thing, you see, though what you can find to tell 'em I can't imagine. But if I'd gone at that pace I should have got right through the Guide Book by this time, and then it would have been all U P, and I should have been obleeged to have invented another dodge. You don't seem to take, Giglamps?'

'Well, I really don't know what you mean,' answered our hero.

'Why,' continued Mr. Bouncer, 'you see, there's only the Mum and Fanny at home; Fanny's my sister, Giglamps — a regular stunner — just suit you! — and they, you understand, don't care to hear about wines, and Town and Gowns, and all that sort of thing; and, you see, I ain't inventive and that, and can't spin a yarn about nothing; so, as soon as ever I came up to Oxford, I invested money in a Guide Book; and I began at the beginning, and I gave the Mum three pages of Guide Book in each letter. Of course, you see, the Mum imagines it's all my own observation; and she thinks no end of my letters, and says that they make her know Oxford almost as well as if she lived here; and she, of course, makes a good deal of me; and as Oxford's the place where I hang out, you see, she takes an interest in reading something about the jolly old place.'

'Of course,' observed Mr. Verdant Green

— 'my mamma — mother, at least — and sisters, always take pleasure in hearing about Oxford; but your plan never occurred to me.'

'It's a first-rater, and no mistake,' said Mr. Bouncer, confidently, 'and saves a deal of trouble. I think of taking out a patent for it — 'Bouncer's Complete Letter-Writer,' — or get some literary swell to put it into a book, 'with a portrait of the inventor;' it would be sure to sell. You see, it's what you call amusement blended with information; and that's more than you can say of most men's letters to the Home department.'

'Cocky Palmer's, for instance,' said Charles Larkyns, 'which always contained a full, true, and particular account of his Wheatley doings. He used to go over there, Verdant, to indulge in the noble sport of cock-fighting, for which he had a most unamiable and unenviable weakness; that was the reason why he was called 'Cocky' Palmer. His elder brother — who was a Pembroke man — was distinguished by the pronomen 'Snuffy,' to express his excessive partiality for that titillating compound.'

'And Snuffy Palmer,' remarked Mr. Bouncer, 'was a long sight better feller than Cocky, who was in the very worst set in Brazenface. But Cocky did the Wheatley dodge once too often, and it was a good job for the King of Oude when his friend Cocky came to grief, and had to take his name off the books.'

'You look as though you wanted a translation of this,' said Charles Larkyns to our hero, who had been listening to the conversation with some wonderment, — understanding about as much of it as many persons who attend the St. James's Theatre understand the dialogue of the French Plays. 'There are College *cabalia*, as well as Jewish; and College surnames are among these. 'The King of Oude' was a man of the name of Towlinson, who always used to carry into Hall with him a bottle of the '*King of Oude's Sauce*,' for which he had some mysterious liking, and without which he professed himself unable to get through his dinner. At one time he was a great friend of Cocky Palmer's, and used to go with him to the cock-fights at Wheatley — that village just on the other side Shotover Hill — where we did a 'constitutional' the other day. Cocky, as our respected friend says, 'Came to grief,' but was allowed to save himself from expulsion by voluntarily, or rather in-voluntarily, taking his name off the books. When his connection with Cocky had thus been ruthlessly broken, 'the King' got into a better set, and retrieved his character.'

'The moral of which, my beloved Giglamps,' observed Mr. Bouncer, 'is that there are as many sets of men in a College as there are of quadrilles in a ball-room, and that it's just as easy to take your place in one as it is in another; but, that when you've once taken up your position, you'll find it ain't an easy thing, you see, to make a change for yourself, till the set is broken up. Whereby, Giglamps, you may comprehend what a grateful bird you ought to be, for Charley's having put you into the best set in Brazenface.'

Mr. Verdant Green was heard to murmur, 'sensible of honour, — grateful for kindness, — endeavours to deserve,' — and the other broken sentiments which are commonly made use of by gentlemen who get upon their legs to return thanks for having been 'tea-potted.'

'If you like to hear it,' said Mr. Bouncer, 'I'll read you my letter to the Mum. It ain't very private; and I flatter myself, Giglamps, that it'll serve you as a model.'

'Let's have it by all means, Harry,' said Charles Larkyns. 'It must be an interesting document; and I am curious to hear what it is that you consider a model for epistolary communication from an undergraduate to his maternal relative.'

'Off she goes then;' observed Mr. Bouncer; 'lend me your ears — list, list, O list! as the recruiting-sergeant or some other feller says in the Play. 'Now, my little dears! look straight for'ard — blow your noses, and don't brathe on the glasses!'' and Mr. Bouncer read the letter, interspersing it with explanatory observations: —

''*My dearest mother, — I have been quite well since I left you, and I hope you and Fanny have been equally salubrious.*' — That's doing the civil, you see: now we pass on to statistics. — '*We had rain the day before yesterday, but we shall have a new moon to-night.*' — You see, the Mum always likes to hear about the weather, so I get that out of the Almanack. Now we get on to the interesting part of the letter. — '*I will now tell you a little about Merton College.*' — That's where I had just got to. We go right through the Guide Book, you understand. — '*The history of this establishment is of peculiar importance, as exhibiting the primary model of all the collegiate bodies in Oxford and Cambridge. The statutes of Walter de Merton had been more or less copied by all other founders in succession; and the whole constitution of both Universities, as we now behold them, may be, not without reason, ascribed to the liberality and munificence of this truly great man.'* — Truly great man! that's no end good, ain't it?' observed Mr. Bouncer, in the manner of the 'mobled queen is good' of Polonius. — '*His sagacity and wisdom led him to profit by the spirit of the times; his opulence enabled him to lay the foundation of a nobler system; and the splendour of his example induced others, in subsequent ages, to raise a superstructure at once attractive and solid.'* — That's piling it up mountaynious, ain't it? — '*The students were no longer dispersed through the streets and lanes of the city, dwelling in insulated houses, halls, inns, or hostels, subject to dubious control and precarious discipline.'* — That's stunnin', isn't it? just like those *Times* fellers write. — '*But placed under the immediate superintendence of tutors and governors, and lodged in comfortable chambers. This was little less than an academical revolution; and a new order of things may be dated from this memorable era. Love to Fanny; and, believe me your affectionate Son, Henry Bouncer.'* — If the Mum don't say that's first-rate, I'm a Dutchman! You see, I don't write very close, so that this respectably fills up three sides of a sheet of note-paper. Oh, here's something over the leaf. '*P.S. I hope Stump and Rowdy have got something for me, because I want some tin very bad*.' That's all! Well, Giglamps! don't you call that quite a model letter for a University man to send to his tender parient?'

'It certainly contains some interesting information,' said our Hero, with a Quaker-like indirectness of reply.

'It seems to me, Harry,' said Charles Larkyns, 'that the pith of it, like a lady's letter, lies in the postscript — the demand for money.'

'You see,' observed the little gentleman in explanation, 'Stump and Rowdy are the beggars that have got all my property till I come of age next year; and they only let me have money at certain times, because it's what they facetiously call *tied-up*: though *why* they've tied it up, or *where* they've tied it up, I haven't the smallest idea. So, though I tick for nearly everything, — for men at College, Giglamps, go upon tick as naturally as the crows do on the sheep's backs, — I sometimes am rather hard up for ready dibs; and then I give the Mum a gentlemanly hint of this, and she tips me. By-the-way,' continued Mr. Bouncer, as he re-read his postscript, 'I must alter the word 'tin' into 'money'; or else she'll be taking it literally, just as she did with the ponies. Know what a pony is, Giglamps?'

'Why, of course I do,' replied Mr. Verdant Green; 'besides which, I have kept one: he was an Exmoor pony, — a bay one, with a long tail.'

'Oh, Giglamps! You'll be the death of me some fine day,' faintly exclaimed little Mr. Bouncer, as he slowly recovered from an exhausting fit of laughter. 'You're as bad as the Mum was. A pony means twenty-five pound, old feller. But the Mum didn't know that; and when I wrote to her and said, 'I'm very short; please to send me two ponies;' meaning, of course, that I wanted fifty pound; what must she do, but write back and say, that, with some difficulty, she had procured for me two Shetland ponies, and that, as I was short, she hoped they would suit my size. And, before I had time to send her another letter, the two little beggars came. Well, I couldn't ride them both at once, like the fellers do at Astley's; so I left one at Tollitt's, and I rode the other down the High, as cool as a cucumber. You see, though I ain't a giant, and that, yet I was big for the pony; and as Shelties are rum-looking little beggars, I dare say we look'd rather queer and original. But the Proctor happened to see me; and he cut up so doosed rough about it, that I couldn't show on the Shelties any more; and Tollitt was obliged to get rid of them for me.'

'Well, Harry,' said Charles Larkyns, 'it is to Tollitt's that you must now go, as you keep your horse there. We want you to join us in a ride.'

'What!' cried out Mr. Bouncer, 'old Giglamps going outside an Oxford hack once more! Why, I thought you'd made a vow never to do so again?'

'Why, I certainly did so,' replied Mr. Verdant Green; 'but Charles Larkyns, during the holidays — the vacation, at least — was kind enough to take me out several rides; so I have had a great deal of practice since last term.'

'And you don't require to be strapped on, or to get inside and pull down the blinds?' inquired Mr. Bouncer.

'Oh dear, no!'

The fact was, that during the long vacation Charles Larkyns had paid considerable attention to our hero's equestrian exercises; not so much, it must be confessed, out of friendship for his friend, as that he might have an opportunity of riding by the side of that friend's fair sister Mary, for whom he entertained something more than a partiality. And herein, probably, Mr. Charles Larkyns showed both taste and judgment. For there may be many things less pleasant in this world than cantering down a green Warwickshire lane — on some soft summer's day when the green is greenest and the blossoms brightest — side by side with a charming girl whose nature is as light and sunny as the summer air and the summer sky. Pleasant it is to watch the flushing cheek glow rosier than the rosiest of all the briar-roses that stoop to kiss it. Pleasant it is to look into the lustrous light of tender eyes; and to see the loosened ringlets reeling with the motion of the ride. Pleasant it is to canter on from lane to lane over soft moss, and springy turf, between the high honey-suckle hedges, and the broad-branched beeches that meet overhead in a tangled embrace. But pleasanter by far than all is it, to hug to one's heart the darling fancy that she who is cantering on by your side in all the witchery of her maiden beauty, holds you in her dearest thoughts, and dowers you with all her wealth of love. Pleasant rides indeed, pleasant fancies, and pleasant day-dreams, had the long vacation brought to Charles Larkyns!

'Well, come along, Verdant,' said Mr. Larkyns, 'we'll go to Charley Symonds' and get our hacks. You can meet us, Harry, just over the Maudlin Bridge; and we'll have a canter along the Henley road.'

So Mr. Verdant Green and his friend walked into Holywell Street, and passed under the archway up to Symonds' stables. But the nervous trepidation which our hero had felt in the same place on a previous occasion returned with full force when his horse was led out in an exuberantly playful and 'fresh' condition. The beast he had bestridden during his long vacation rides, with his sister and his (and sister's) friend, was a cob-like steed, whose placidity of temper was fully equalled by its gravity of demeanour; and who would as soon have thought of flying over a five-bar gate as he would of kicking up his respectable heels both behind and before in the low-lived manner recorded of the Ethiopian 'Old Joe.' But, if 'Charley Symonds'' hacks had been of this pacific and easygoing kind, it is highly probable that Mr. C. S. and his stud would not have acquired that popularity which they had deservedly achieved. For it seems to be a *sine-qua-non* with an Oxford hack, that to general showiness of exterior, it must add the power of enduring any amount of hard riding and rough treatment in the course of the day which its *pro-tem* proprietor may think fit to inflict upon it; it being an axiom which has obtained, as well in Universities as in other places, that it is of no advantage to hire a hack unless you get out of him as much as you can for your money; you won't want to use him to-morrow, so you don't care about over-riding him to-day.

But, all this time, Mr. Verdant Green is drawing on his gloves, in the nervous manner that tongue-tied gentlemen go through the same performance during the conversational spasms of the first-set of Quadrilles; the groom is leading out the exuberantly playful quadruped on whose back Mr. Verdant Green is to disport himself; Charles Larkyns is mounted; the November sun is shining brightly on the perspective of the yard and stables, and the tower of New College; the dark archway gives one a peep of Holywell Street; while the cold blue sky is flecked with gleaming pigeons. At last, Mr. Verdant Green has scrambled into his saddle, and is riding cautiously down the yard, while his heart beats in an alarming alarum-like way. As they ride under the archway, there, in the little room underneath it, is Mr. Four-in-hand

Fosbrooke, selecting his particular tandem-whip from a group of some two score of similar whips kept there in readiness for their respective owners.

'Charley, you're a beast!' says Mr. Fosbrooke, politely addressing himself to Mr. Larkyns; 'I wanted Bouncer to come with me in the cart to Abingdon, and I find that the little man is engaged to you.' Upon which, Mr. Fosbrooke playfully raising his tandem-whip, Mr. Verdant Green's horse plunges, and brings his rider's head into concussion with the lamp which hangs within the gateway; whereupon, the hat falls off, and our hero is within an ace of following his hat's example. By a powerful exertion, however, he recovers his proper position in the saddle, and proceeds in an agitated and jolted condition, by Charles Larkyns's side, down Holywell Street, past the Music Room, and round by the Long Wall, and over Magdalen Bridge. Here they are soon joined by Mr. Bouncer, mounted, according to the custom of small men, on one of Tollitt's tallest horses, of ever-so-many hands high. As by this time our hero has got more accustomed to his steed, his courage gradually returns, and he rides on with his companions very pleasantly, enjoying the magnificent distant view of his University. When they have passed Cowley, some very tempting fences are met with; and Mr. Bouncer and Mr. Larkyns, being unable to resist their fascinations, put their horses at them, and leap in and out of the road in an insane Vandycking kind of way; while an excited agriculturist, whose smock-frock heaves with indignation, pours down denunciations on their heads.

'Blow that bucolical party!' says Mr. Bouncer; 'he's no right to interfere with the enjoyments of the animals. If they break the fences, it ain't their faults; it's the fault of the farmers for not making the fences strong enough to bear them. Come along, Giglamps! put your beast at that hedge! he'll take you over as easy as if you were sitting in an arm-chair.'

But Mr. Verdant Green has doubts about the performance of this piece of equestrian upholstery; and, thinking that the arm-chair would soon become a reclining one, he is firm in his refusal to put the leaping powers of his steed to the test. But having, afterwards, obtained some 'jumping powder' at a certain small road-side hostelry to which Mr. Bouncer has piloted the party, our hero, on his way back to Oxford, screws up his courage sufficiently to gallop his steed desperately at a ditch which yawns, a foot wide, before him. But to his immense astonishment — not to say, disgust — the obtuse-minded quadruped gives a leap which would have taken him clear over a canal; and our hero, not being prepared for this very needless display of agility, flies off the saddle at a tangent, and finds that his 'vaulting ambition' had o'erleap'd itself, and fallen on the other side — of the ditch.

'It ain't your fault, Giglamps!' says Mr. Bouncer, when he has galloped after Verdant's steed, and has led it up to him, and when he has ascertained that his friend is not in the least hurt; but has only broken — his glasses; 'it ain't your fault, Giglamps, old feller! it's the clumsiness of the hack. He tossed you up, and couldn't catch you again!'

And so our hero rides back to Oxford. But, before the Term has ended, he has become more accustomed to Oxford hacks, and has made himself acquainted with the respective merits of the stables of Messrs. Symonds, Tollitt, and Pigg; and has, moreover, ridden with the drag, and, in this way, hunted the fabled foxes of Bagley Wood, and Whichwood Forest.

6

Mr. Verdant Green Feathers his Oars with Skill and Dexterity

November is not always the month of fog and mist and dullness. Oftentimes there are brilliant exceptions to that generally-received rule of depressing weather which, in this month (according to our lively neighbours), induces the natives of our English metropolis to leap in crowds from the Bridge of Waterloo. There are in November, days of calm beauty, which are peculiar to that month — that kind of calm beauty which is so often seen as the herald of decay.

But, whatever weather the month may bring to Oxford, it never brings gloom or despondency to Oxford men. They are a happily constituted set of beings, and can always create their own amusements; they crown Minerva with flowers without heeding her influenza, and never seem to think that the rosy-bosomed Hours may be laid up with bronchitis. Winter and summer appear to be pretty much the same to them: reading and recreation go hand-in-hand all the year round; and, among other pleasures, that of boating finds as many votaries in cold November, as it did in sunny June — indeed, the chillness of the air, in the former month, gives zest to an amusement which degenerates to hard labour in the dog-days.

The classic Isis in the month of November, therefore, whenever the weather is anything like favourable, presents an animated scene. Eight-oars pass along, the measured pull of the oars in the rowlocks marking the time in musical cadence with their plashing dip in the water; perilous skiffs flit like fire-flies over the glassy surface of the river; men lounge about in the house-boats and barges, or gather together at King's, or Hall's, and industriously promulgate small talk and tobacco-smoke. All is gay and bustling. Although the feet of the strollers in the Christ Church meadows rustle through the sere and yellow leaf, yet rich masses of brown and russet foliage still hang upon the trees, and light up into gold in the sun. The sky is of a cold but bright blue; the distant hills and woods are mellowed into sober purplish-gray tints, but over them the sun looks down with that peculiar red glow which is only seen in November.

It was one of these bright days of 'the

month of gloom,' that Mr. Verdant Green and Mr. Charles Larkyns being in the room of their friend Mr. Bouncer, the little gentleman inquired, 'Now then! what are you two fellers up to? I'm game for anything, I am! from pitch-and-toss to manslaughter.'

'I'm afraid,' said Charles Larkyns, 'that we can't accommodate you in either amusement, although we are going down to the river, with which Verdant wishes to renew his acquaintance. Last term, you remember, you picked him up in the Gut, when he had been played with at pitch-and-toss in a way that very nearly resembled manslaughter.'

'I remember, I remember, how old Giglamps floated by!' said Mr. Bouncer; 'you looked like a half-bred mermaid Giglamps.'

'But the gallant youth,' continued Mr. Larkyns, 'undismayed by the perils from which he was then happily preserved, has boldly come forward and declared himself a worshipper of Isis, in a way worthy of the ancient Egyptians, or of Tom Moore's Epicurean.'

'Well! stop a minute you fellers,' said Mr. Bouncer; 'I must have my beer first: I can't do without my Bass relief. I'm like the party in the old song, and I likes a drop of good beer.' And as he uncorked a bottle of Bass, little Mr. Bouncer sang, in notes as musical as those produced from his own tin horn —

‘’Twixt wet and dry I always try
Between the extremes to steer;
Though I always shrunk from getting
— *intoxicated*,
I was always fond of my beer!

For I likes a drop of good beer!
I’m particularly partial to beer!
Porter and swipes
Always give me the — *stomach-ache*!
But that’s never the case with beer!’

‘Bravo, Harry!’ cried Charles Larkyns; ‘you roar us an’ twere any nightingale. It would do old Bishop Still’s heart good to hear you; and ‘sure *I* think, that *you* can drink with any that wears a hood,’ or that *will* wear a hood when you take your Bachelor’s, and put on your gown.’ And Charles Larkyns sang, rather more musically than Mr. Bouncer had done, from that song which, three centuries ago, the Bishop had written in praise of good ale —

Let back and side go bare, go bare,
Both hand and foot go cold:
But, belly, God send thee good ale
enough,
Whether it be new or old.

They were soon down at the river side, where Verdant was carefully put into a tub (alas! the dear, awkward, safe, old things are fast passing away; they are giving place to suicidal skiffs, and will soon be numbered among the boats of other days!) — and was started off with almost as much difficulty as on his first essay. The tub — which was, indeed, his old friend the *Sylph*, — betrayed an awkward propensity for veering round towards Folly Bridge, which our hero at first failed to overcome; and it was not until he had performed a considerable amount of crab-catching, that he was enabled to steer himself in the proper direction. Charles Larkyns had taken his seat in an outrigger skiff (so frail and shaky that it made Verdant nervous to look at it), and, with one or two powerful strokes, had shot ahead, backed water, turned, and pulled back round the tub long before Verdant had succeeded in passing that eccentric mansion, to which allusion has before been made, as possessing in the place of cellars, an ingenious system of small rivers to thoroughly irrigate its foundation — a hydropathic treatment which may (or may not) be agreeable in Venice, but strikes one as being decidedly cold and comfortless when applied to Oxford, — at any rate, in the month of November. Walking on the lawn which stretched from this house towards the river, our hero espied two extremely pretty young ladies, whose hearts he endeavoured at once to take captive by displaying all his powers in that elegant exercise in which they saw him engaged. It may reasonably be presumed that Mr. Verdant Green's hopes were doomed to be blighted.

Let us leave him, and take a look at Mr. Bouncer.

Mr. Bouncer had been content to represent the prowess of his college in the cricket-field, and had never aspired to any fame as an oar. The exertions, as well as the fame, of aquatic honours, he had left to Mr. Blades, and those others like him, who considered it a trifle to pull down to Iffley and back again, two or three times a day, at racing pace with a fresh spurt put on every five minutes.

Mr. Bouncer, too, had an antipathy to eat beefsteaks otherwise than in the state in which they are usually brought to table; and, as it seemed a *sine qua non* with the gentleman who superintended the training for the boat-races, that his pupils should daily devour beefsteaks which had merely looked at the fire, Mr. Bouncer, not having been brought up to cannibal habits, was unable to conform himself to this, and those other vital principles which seemed to regulate the science of aquatic training. The little gentleman moreover, did not join with the 'Torpids' (as the second boats of a college are called), either, because he had a soul above them, — he would be *aut Caesar, aut nullus*; either in the eight, or nowhere, — or else, because even the Torpids would cause him more trouble and pleasurable pain than would be agreeable to him. When Mr. Bouncer sat down on any hard substance, he liked to be able to do so without betraying any emotion that the action caused him personal discomfort; and he had noticed that many of the Torpids — not to mention one or two of the eight — were more particular than young men usually are about having a very easy, soft, and yielding chair to sit on.

Mr. Bouncer, too, was of opinion that continued blisters were both unsightly and unpleasant; and that rawness was bad enough when taken in conjunction with beefsteaks, without being extended to one's own hands. He had also a summer passion for ices and creams, which were forbidden luxuries to one in training, — although (paradoxical as it may seem to say so) they trained on Isis! He had also acquired a bad habit of getting up in one day, and going to bed in the next, — keeping late hours, and only rising early when absolutely compelled to do so in order to keep morning chapel — a habit which the trainer would have interfered with, considerably to the little gentleman's advantage. He had also an amiable weakness for pastry, port, claret, 'et *hock* genus omne'; and would have felt it a cruelty to have been deprived of his daily modicum of 'smoke'; and in all these points, boat-training would have materially interfered with his comfort.

Mr. Bouncer, therefore, amused himself equally as much to his own satisfaction as if he had been one of the envied eight, by occasionally paddling about with Charles Larkyns in an old pair-oar, built by Davis and King, and bought by Mr. Bouncer of its late Brazenfacian proprietor, when that gentleman, after a humorous series of plucks, rustications, and heavy debts, had finally been compelled to migrate to the King's Bench, for that purification of purse and person commonly designated 'whitewashing.' When Charles Larkyns and his partner did not use their pair-oar, the former occupied his outrigger skiff; and the latter, taking Huz and Buz on board a sailing boat, tacked up and down the river with great skill, the smoke gracefully curling from his meerschaum or short black pipe, — for Mr. Bouncer disapproved of smoking cigars at those times when the wind would have assisted him to get through them.

'Hullo, Giglamps! here we are! as the clown says in the pantermime,' sung out the little gentleman as he came up with our hero, who was performing some extraordinary feats in full sight of the University crew, who were just starting from their barge; 'you get no end of exercise out of your tub, I should think, by the style you work those paddles. They go in and out beautiful! Splish, splash; splish, splash! You must be one of the *wherry* identical Row-brothers-row, whose voices kept tune and whose ears kept time, you know. You ought to go and splish-splash in the Freshman's River, Giglamps; — but I forgot — you ain't a Freshman now, are you, old feller? Those swells in the University boats look as though they were bursting with envy — not to say, with laughter,' added Mr. Bouncer, *sotto voce*. 'Who taught you to do the dodge in such a stunning way, Giglamps?'

'Why, last term, Charles Larkyns did,' responded Mr. Verdant Green, with the freshness of a Freshman still lingering lovingly upon him. 'I've not forgotten what he told me, — to put in my oar deep, and to bring it out with a jerk. But though I make them go as deep as I can, and jerk them out as much as possible, yet the boat *will* keep turning round, and I can't keep it straight at all; and the oars are very heavy and unmanageable, and keep slipping out of the rowlocks — '

'Commonly called *rullocks*,' put in Mr. Bouncer, as a parenthetical correction, or marginal note on Mr. Verdant Green's words.

'And when the Trinity boat went by, I could scarcely get out of their way; and they said very unpleasant things to me; and, altogether, I can assure you that it has made me very hot.'

'And a capital thing, too, Giglamps, this cold November day,' said Mr. Bouncer; 'I'm obliged to keep my coppers warm with this pea-coat, and my pipe. Charley came alongside me just now, on purpose to fire off one of his poetical quotations. He said that I reminded him of Beattie's *Minstrel*: —

> 'Dainties he needed not, nor gaud, nor toy,
> Save one short pipe.'

'I think that was something like it. But you see, Giglamps, I haven't got a figure-head for these sort of things like Charley has, so I couldn't return his shot; but since then, to me deeply pondering, as those old Greek parties say, a fine sample of our superior old crusted jokes has come to hand; and when Charley next pulls alongside, I shall tell him that I am like that beggar we read about in old Slowcoach's lecture the other day, and that, if I had been in the humour, I could have sung out, Io Bacche! *I owe baccy* — d'ye see, Giglamps? Well, old feller! you look rather puffed, so clap on your coat; and, if there's a rope's end, or a chain, in your tub, and you'll just pay it out here, I'll make you fast astern, and pull you down the river; and then you'll be in prime condition to work yourself up again. The wind's in our back, and we shall get on jolly.'

So our hero made fast the tub to his friend's sailing-boat, and was towed as far as the Haystack. During the voyage Mr. Bouncer ascertained that Mr. Charles Larkyns had improved some of the shining hours of the long vacation considerably to Mr. Verdant Green's benefit, by teaching him the art of swimming — a polite accomplishment of which our hero had been hitherto ignorant. Little Mr. Bouncer, therefore, felt easier in his mind, if any repetition of his involuntary bath in the Gut should befal our hero; and, after giving him (wonderful to say) some correct advice regarding the management of the oars, he cast off the *Sylph*, and left her and our hero to their own devices. But, profiting by the friendly hints which he had received, Mr. Verdant Green made considerable progress in the skill and dexterity with which he feathered his oars; and he sat in his tub looking as wise as Diogenes may (perhaps) have done in *his*. He moreover pulled the boat back to Hall's without meeting with any accident worth mentioning; and when he had got on shore he was highly complimented by Mr. Blades and a group of boating gentlemen 'for the admirable display of science which he had afforded them.'

Mr. Verdant Green was afterwards taken alternately by Charles Larkyns and Mr. Bouncer in their pair-oar; so that, by the end of the term, he at any rate knew more of boating than to accept as one of its fundamental rules, 'put your oar in deep, and bring it out with a jerk.'

In the first week in December he had an opportunity of pulling over a fresh piece of water. One of those inundations occurred to which Oxford is so liable, and the meadowland to the south and west of the city was covered by the flood. Boats plied to and from the railway station in place of omnibuses; the Great Western was not to be seen for water; and, at the Abingdon-road bridge, at Cold-harbour, the rails were washed away, and the trains brought to a stand-still. The Isis was amplified to the width of the Christ

Church meadows; the Broad Walk had a peep of itself upside down in the glassy mirror; the windings of the Cherwell could only be traced by the trees on its banks. There was

'Water, water everywhere,'

and a disagreeable quantity of it too, as those Christ Church men whose ground-floor rooms were towards the meadows soon discovered.

Mr. Bouncer is supposed to have brought out one of his 'fine, old, crusted jokes,' when he asserted in reference to the inundation, that 'Nature had assumed a lake complexion.' Posts and rails, and hay, and a miscellaneous collection of articles, were swept along by the current, together with the bodies of hapless sheep and pigs. But, in spite of these incumbrances, boats of all descriptions were to be seen sailing, pulling, skiffing, and punting, over the flooded meadows. Numerous were the disasters, and many were the boats that were upset.

Indeed, the adventures of Mr. Verdant Green would probably have here terminated in a misadventure, had he not (thanks to Charles Larkyns) mastered the art of swimming; for he was in Mr. Bouncer's sailing-boat, which was sailing very merrily over the flood, when its merriness was suddenly checked by its grounding on the stump of a lopped pollard willow, and forthwith capsizing. Our hero, who had been sitting in the bows, was at once swept over by the sail, and, for a moment, was in great peril; but, disengaging himself from the cordage, he struck out, and swam to a willow whose friendly boughs and top had just formed an asylum for Mr. Bouncer, who in great anxiety was coaxing Huz and Buz to swim to the same ark of safety.

Mr. Verdant Green and Mr. Bouncer were speedily rescued from their position, and were not a little thankful for their escape.

7

Mr. Verdant Green Partakes of a Dove-Tart and a Spread-Eagle

'Hullo, Giglamps, you lazy beggar!' said the cheery voice of little Mr. Bouncer, as he walked into our hero's bedroom one morning towards the end of term, and found Mr. Verdant Green in bed, though sufficiently awakened by the sounding of Mr. Bouncer's octaves for the purposes of conversation; 'this'll never do, you know, Giglamps! Cutting chapel to do the downy! Why, what do you mean, sir? Didn't you ever learn in the nursery what happened to old Daddy Longlegs when he wouldn't say his prayers?'

'Robert *did* call me,' said our hero, rubbing his eyes; 'but I felt tired, so I told him to put in an *aeger*.'

'Upon my word, young un,' observed Mr. Bouncer, 'you're a coming it, you are! and only in your second term, too. What makes you wear a nightcap, Giglamps? Is it to make your hair curl, or to keep your venerable head warm? Nightcaps ain't healthy; they are only fit for long-tailed babbies, and old birds that are as bald as coots; or else for gents that grease their wool with 'thine incomparable oil, Macassar,' as the noble poet justly remarks.

'It ain't always pleasant,' continued the little gentleman, who was perched up on the side of the bed, and seemed in a communicative disposition, 'it ain't always pleasant to turn out for morning chapel, is it, Giglamps? But it's just like the eels with their skinning: it goes against the grain at first, but you soon get used to it. When I first came up, I was a frightful lazy beggar, and I got such a heap of impositions for not keeping my morning chapels, that I was obliged to have three fellers constantly at work writing 'em out for me. This was rather expensive, you see; and then the dons threatened to take away my term altogether, and bring me to grief, if I didn't be more regular. So I was obliged to make a virtuous resolution, and I told Robert that he was to insist on my getting up in a morning, and I should tip him at the end of term if he succeeded. So at first he used to come and hammer at the door; but that was no go. So then he used to come in and shake me, and try to pull the clothes off; but, you see, I always used to prepare for him, by taking a good supply of boots and things to bed with me; so I was able to take shies at the beggar till he vanished, and left me to snooze peaceably. You see, it ain't every feller as likes to have a Wellington boot at his head; but that rascal of a Robert is used to those trifles, and I was obliged to try another dodge. This you know was only of a morning when I was in bed. When I had had my breakfast, and got my imposition, and become virtuous again, I used to slang him awful for having let me cut chapel; and then I told him that he must always stand at the door until he heard me out of bed. But, when the morning came, it seemed running such a risk, you see, to one's lungs and all those sort of things to turn out of the warm bed into the cold chapel, that I would answer Robert when he hammered at the door; but, instead of getting up, I would knock my boots against the floor, as though I was out of bed, don't you see, and was padding about. But that wretch of a Robert was too old a bird to be caught with this dodge; so he used to sing out, 'You must show a leg, sir!' and, as he kept on hammering at the door till I *did* — for, you see, Giglamps, he was looking out for the tip at the end of term, so it made him persevere — and as his beastly hammering used, of course, to put a stopper on my going to sleep again, I used to rush out in a frightful state of wax, and show a leg. And then, being well up, you see, it was no use doing the downy again, so it was just as well to make one's *twilight* and go to chapel. Don't gape, Giglamps; it's beastly rude, and I haven't done yet. I'm going to tell you another dodge — one of old Smalls'. He invested money in an alarum, with a string from it tied on to the bed-clothes, so as to pull them off at whatever time you chose to set it. But I never saw the fun of being left high and dry on your bed: it would be a shock to the system which I couldn't stand. But even this dreadful expedient would be better than posting an *aeger*; which, you know, you didn't ought to was, Giglamps. Well, turn out, old feller! I've told Robert to take your commons into my room. Smalls and Charley are coming, and I've got a dove-tart and a spread-eagle.'

'Whatever are they?' asked Mr. Verdant Green.

'Not know what they are!' cried Mr. Bouncer; 'why a dove-tart is what mortals call a pigeon-pie. I ain't much in Tennyson's line, but it strikes me that dove-tarts are more poetical than the other thing; spread-eagle is a barn-door fowl smashed out flat, and made jolly with mushroom sauce, and no end of good things. I don't know how they squash it, but I should say that they sit upon it; I daresay, if we were to inquire, we should find that they kept a fat feller on purpose. But you just come, and try how it eats.' And, as Mr. Verdant Green's bedroom barely afforded standing room, even for one, Mr. Bouncer walked into the sitting-room, while his friend arose from his couch like a youthful Adonis, and proceeded to bathe his ambrosial person, by taking certain sanatory measures in splashing about in a species of tub — a performance which Mr. Bouncer was wont to term 'doing tumbies.'

'What'll you take for your letters, Giglamps?' called out the little gentleman from the other room; 'the Post's in, and here are three for you. Two are from women, — young 'uns I should say, from the regular ups and downs, and right angles: they look like billyduxes. Give you a bob for them, at a venture! they may be funny. The other is suspiciously like a tick, and ought to be looked shy on. I should advise you not to open it, but to pitch it in the fire: it may save a fit of the blues. If you want any help over shaving, just say so, Giglamps, will you, before I go; and then I'll hold your nose for you, or do anything else that's civil and accommodating. And, when you've done your tumbies, come in to the dove-tart and the spread-eagle.' And off went Mr. Bouncer, making terrible noises with his post-horn, in his strenuous but futile endeavours to discover the octaves.

Our hero soon concluded his 'tumbies' and his dressing (*not* including the shaving), and made his way to Mr. Bouncer's rooms, where he did full justice to the dove-tart, and admired the spread-eagle so much, that he thought of bribing the confectioner for the recipe to take home as a Christmas-box for his mother.

'Well, Giglamps,' said Mr. Bouncer, when breakfast was over, 'to spare the blushes on your venerable cheeks, I won't even so much as refer to the billyduxes; but, I'll only ask, what was the damage of the tick?'

'Oh! it was not a bill,' replied Mr. Verdant Green; 'it was a letter about a dog from the man of whom I bought Mop last term.'

'What! Filthy Lucre?' cried Mr. Bouncer; 'well, I thought, somehow, I knew the fist! he writes just as if he'd learnt from imitating his dogs' hind-legs. Let's have a sight of it if it ain't private and confidential!'

'Oh dear no! on the contrary, I was going to show it to you, and ask your advice on the contents.' And Verdant handed to Mr. Bouncer a letter, which had been elaborately sealed with the aid of a key, and was directed high up in the left-hand corner to

> 'Virdon grene esqre braisenface collidge Oxford.'

'You look beastly lazy, Charley!' said Mr. Bouncer to Mr. Charles Larkyns; 'so, while I fill my pipe, just spit out the letter, *pro bono*.' And Charles Larkyns, lying in Mr. Bouncer's easiest lounging chair, read as follows: —

> 'Onnerd sir i tak the libbaty of a Dressin of you in respex of A dog which i wor sorry For to ear of your Loss in mop which i had The pleshur of Sellin of 2 you onnerd sir A going astray And not a turnin hup Bein of A unsurtin Tempor and guv to A folarin of strandgers which wor maybe as ow You wor a lusein on him onnerd Sir bein Overdogd at this ere present i can let you have A rale good teryer at A barrging which wold giv sattefacshun onnered Sir it wor 12 munth ago i Sold to Bounser esqre a red smooth air terier Dog anserin 2 nam of Tug as wor rite down goodun and No mistake onnerd Sir the purpurt Of this ere is too say as ow i have a Hone brother to Tug black tann and ful ears and If you wold like him i shold bee prowd too wate on you onnerd Sir he wor by robbingsons Twister out of

mister jones of abingdons Fan of witch brede Bounser esqre nose on the merritts onnerd Sir he is very Smal and smooth air and most xlent aither for wood Or warter a liter before Tug onnerd Sir is nam is Vermin and he hant got his nam by no mistake as No Vermin not even poll katts can live long before him onnerd Sir I considders as vermin is very sootble compannion for a Gent indors or hout and bein lively wold give amoosement i shall fele it A plesure a waitin on you onnerd Sir opin you will pardin the libbaty of a Dressin of you but my head wor ful of vermin and i wishd to tel you

'onnerd Sir yures 2 komand j. Looker.'

'The nasty beggar!' said Mr. Bouncer, in reference to the last paragraph. 'Well, Giglamps! Filthy Lucre doesn't tell fibs when he says that Tug came of a good breed: but he was so doosed pugnacious, that he was always having set-to's with Huz and Buz, in the coal-shop just outside the door here; and so, as I'd nowhere else to stow them, I was obliged to give Tug away. Dr. What's-his-name says, 'Let dogs delight to bark and bite, for 'tis their nature to.' But then, you see, it's only a delight when they bite *somebody else's* dog; and if Dr. What's-his-name had had a kennel of his own, he wouldn't have took it so coolly; and, whether it was their nature so to do or not, he wouldn't have let the little beggars, that he fork'd out thirteen bob a-year for to the government, amuse themselves by biting each other, or tearing out each other's eyes; he'd have turn'd them over, don't you see, to his neighbours' dogs, and have let them do the biting department on *them*. And, altogether, Giglamps, I'd advise you to let Filthy Lucre's Vermin alone, and have nothing to do with the breed.'

So Mr. Verdant Green took his friend's advice, and then took himself off to learn boxing at the hands, and gloves, of the Putney Pet; for our hero, at the suggestion of Mr. Charles Larkyns, had thought it advisable to receive a few lessons in the fistic art, in order that he might be the better able to defend himself, should he be engaged in a second Town and Gown. He found the Pet in attendance upon Mr. Foote; and, by their mutual aid, speedily mastered the elements of the Art of Self-defence.

Mr. Foote's rooms at St. John's were in the further corner to the right-hand side of the Quad, and had windows looking into the gardens. When Charles had held his Court at St. John's, and when the loyal College had melted down its plate to coin into money for the King's necessities, the Royal visitor had occupied these very rooms. But it was not on this account alone that they were the show rooms of the College, and that tutors sent their compliments to Mr. Foote, with the request that he would allow a party of friends to see his rooms. It was chiefly on account of the lavish manner in which Mr. Foote had furnished his rooms, with what he theatrically called 'properties,' that made them so sought out: and country lionisers of Oxford, who took their impressions of an Oxford student's room from those of Mr. Foote, must have entertained very highly coloured ideas of the internal aspect of the sober-looking old Colleges.

The sitting-room was large and lofty, and was panelled with oak throughout. At the further end was an elaborately carved book-case of walnut wood, filled with books gorgeously bound in every tint of morocco and vellum, with their backs richly tooled in gold. It was currently reported in the College that 'Footelights' had given an order for a certain number of *feet* of books, — not being at all proud as to their contents, — and had laid down the sum of a thousand pounds (or thereabouts) for their binding. This might have been scandal; but the fact of his father being a Colossus of (the iron) Roads, and indulging his son and heir in every expense, gave some colour to the rumour.

The panels were covered with the choicest engravings (all proofs-before-letters), and with water-colour drawings by Cattermole, Cox, Fripp, Hunt, and Frederick Tayler — their wide, white margins being sunk in light gilt frames. Above these gleamed groups of armour, standing out effectively (and theatrically), against the dark oak panels, and full of 'reflected lights,' that would have gladdened the heart of Maclise. There were couches of velvet, and lounging chairs of every variety and shape. There was a Broadwood's grand pianoforte, on which Mr. Foote, although uninstructed, could play skilfully. There were round tables and square tables, and writing tables; and there were side tables with statuettes, and Swiss carvings, and old china, and gold apostle-spoons, and lava ware, and Etruscan vases, and a swarm of Spiers's elegant knick-knackeries. There were reading-stands of all sorts; Briarean-armed brazen ones that fastened on to the chair you sat in, — sloping ones to rest on the table before you, elaborately carved in open work, and an upright one of severe Gothic, like a lectern, where you were to stand and read without contracting your chest. Then there were all kinds of stands to hold books: sliding ones, expanding ones, portable ones, heavy fixture ones, plain mahogany ones, and oak ones made glorious by Margetts with the arms of Oxford and St. John's, carved and emblazoned on the ends.

Mr. Foote's rooms were altogether a very gorgeous instance of a Collegian's apartment; and Mr. Foote himself was a very striking example of the theatrical undergraduate. Possessing great powers of mimicry and facial expression, he was able to imitate any peculiarities which were to be observed either in Dons or Undergraduates, in Presidents or Scouts. He could sit down at his piano, and give you — after the manner of Theodore Hook, or John Parry — a burlesque opera; singing high up in his head for the prima donna, and going down to his boots for the *basso profondo* of the great Lablache. He could also draw corks, saw wood, do a bee in a handkerchief, and make monkeys, cats, dogs, a farm-yard, or a full band, with equal facility. He would also give you Mr. Keeley, in 'Betsy Baker;' Mr. Paul Bedford, as 'I believe you my bo-o-oy'; Mr. Buckstone, as Cousin Joe, and 'Box and Cox;' or Mr. Wright, as Paul Pry, or Mr. Felix Fluffy. Besides the comedians, Mr. Footelights would also give you the leading tragedians, and would favour you (through his nose) with the popular burlesque imitation of Mr. Charles Kean, as *Hablet*. He would fling himself down on the carpet, and grovel there as Hamlet does in the play-scene, and would exclaim, with frantic vehemence, 'He poisods hib i' the garded, for his estate. His dabe's Godzago: the story is extadt, ad writted id very choice Italiad. You shall see adod, how the burderer gets the love of Godzago's wife.' Moreover, as his room possessed the singularity of a trap-door leading down into a wine-cellar, Mr. 'Footelights' was thus enabled to leap down into the aperture, and carry on the personation of Hamlet in Ophelia's grave. As the theatrical trait in his character was productive of much amusement, and as he was also considered to be one of those hilarious fragments of masonry, popularly known as 'jolly bricks,' Mr. Foote's society was greatly cultivated; and Mr. Verdant Green struck up a warm friendship with him.

But the Michaelmas term was drawing to its close. Buttery and kitchen books were adding up their sums total; bursars were preparing for battels; witless men were cramming for Collections; scouts and bedmakers were looking for tips; and tradesmen were hopelessly expecting their little accounts. And, in a few days, Mr. Verdant Green might have been seen at the railway station, in company with

Mr. Charles Larkyns and Mr. Bouncer, setting out for the Manor Green, *via* London — this being, as is well known, the most direct route from Oxford to Warwickshire.

Mr. Bouncer, who when travelling was never easy in his mind unless Huz and Buz were with him in the same carriage, had placed these two interesting specimens of the canine species in a small light box, partially ventilated by means of holes drilled through the top. But Huz and Buz, not much admiring this contracted mode of conveyance, and probably suffering from incipient asphyxia, in spite of the admonitory kicks against their box, gave way to dismal howls, at the very moment when the guard came to look at the tickets.

'Can't allow dogs in here, sir! they must go in the locker,' said the guard.

'Dogs?' cried Mr. Bouncer, in apparent astonishment: 'they're rabbits!'

'Rabbits!' ejaculated the guard, in his turn. 'Oh, come, sir! what makes rabbits bark?'

'What makes 'em bark? Why, because they've got the pip, poor beggars!' replied Mr. Bouncer, promptly. At which the guard graciously laughed, and retired; probably thinking that he should, in the end, be a gainer if he allowed Huz and Buz to journey in the same first-class carriage with their master.

8

Mr. Verdant Green Spends a Merry Christmas and a Happy New Year

Christmas had come; the season of kindness, and hospitality; the season when the streams of benevolence flow full in their channels; the season when the Honourable Miss Hyems indulges herself with ice, while the vulgar Jack Frost regales himself with cold-without. Christmas had come, and had brought with it an old fashioned winter; and, as Mr. Verdant Green stands with his hands in his pockets, and gazes from the drawing-room of his paternal mansion, he looks forth upon a white world.

The snow is everywhere. The shrubs are weighed down by masses of it; the terrace is knee-deep in it; the plaster Apollo, in the long-walk, is more than knee-deep in it, and is furnished with a surplice and wig, like a half-blown Bishop. The distant country looks the very ghost of a landscape: the white-walled cottages seem part and parcel of the snow-drifts around them, — drifts that take every variety of form, and are swept by the wind into faery wreaths, and fantastic caves. The old mill-wheel is locked fast, and gemmed with giant icicles; its slippery stairs are more slippery than ever. Golden gorse and purple heather are now all of a colour; orchards put forth blossoms of real snow; the gently swelling hills look bright and dazzling in the wintry sun; the grey church tower has grown from grey to white; nothing looks black, except the swarms of rooks that dot the snowy fields, or make their caws (long as any Chancery-suit) to be heard from among the dark branches of the stately elms that form the avenue to the Manor Green.

It is a rare busy time for the intelligent Mr. Mole the gardener! he is always sweeping at that avenue, and, do what he will, he cannot keep it clear from snow. As Mr. Verdant Green looks forth upon the white world, his gaze is more particularly directed to this avenue, as though the form of the intelligent Mr. Mole was an object of interest. From time to time Mr. Verdant Green consults his watch in a nervous manner, and is utterly indifferent to the appeals of the robin-redbreast who is hopping about outside, in expectation of the dinner which has been daily given to him.

Just when the robin, emboldened by

hunger, has begun to tap fiercely with his bill against the window-pane, as a gentle hint that the smallest donations of crumbs of comfort will be thankfully received, — Mr. Verdant Green, utterly oblivious of robins in general, and of the sharp pecks of this one in particular, takes no notice of the little redbreast waiter with the bill, but, slightly colouring up, fixes his gaze upon the lodge-gate through which a group of ladies and gentlemen are passing. Stepping back for a moment, and stealing a glance at himself in the mirror, Mr. Verdant Green hurriedly arranges and disarranges his hair — pulls about his collar — ties and unties his neck-handkerchief — buttons and then unbuttons his coat — takes another look from the window — sees the intelligent Mr. Mole, (besom in hand) salaaming the party, and then makes a rush for the vestibule, to be at the door to receive them.

Let us take a look at them as they come up the avenue. *Place aux dames*, is the proper sort of thing; but as there is no rule without its exception, and no adage without its counter-proverb, we will give the gentlemen the priority of description.

Hale and hearty, the picture of amiability and gentlemanly feeling, comes the Rector, Mr. Larkyns, sturdily crunching the frozen snow, which has defied all the besom powers of the intelligent Mr. Mole. Here, too, is Mr. Charles Larkyns, and, moreover, his friend Henry Bouncer, Esq., who has come to christmas at the Rectory. Following in their wake is a fourth gentleman attired in the costume peculiar to clergymen, dissenting ministers, linen-drapers' assistants, and tavern waiters. He happens to belong to the first-named section, and is no less a person than the Rev. Josiah Meek, B.A., (St. Christopher's Coll., Oxon.) — who, for the last three months, has officiated as Mr. Larkyns's curate. He appears to be of a peace-loving, lamb-like disposition; and, though sportive as a lamb when occasion requires, is yet of timid ways and manners. He is timid, too, in voice, — speaking in a feeble treble; he is timid, too, in his address, — more particularly as regards females; and he has mild-looking whiskers, that are far too timid to assume any decided or obtrusive colour, and have fallen back on a generalized whitey-brown tint. But, though timid enough in society, he was bold and energetic in the discharge of his pastoral duties, and had already won the esteem of every one in the parish. So, Verdant had been told, when, on his return from college, he had asked his sisters how they liked the new curate. They had not only heard of his good deeds, but they had witnessed many of them in their visits to the schools and among the poor. Mary and Fanny were loud in his praise; and if Helen said but little, it was perhaps because she thought the more; for Helen was now of the susceptible age of 'sweet seventeen,' an age that not only feels warmly but thinks deeply; and, who shall say what feelings and thoughts may lie beneath the pure waters of that sea of maidenhood whose surface is so still and calm? Love alone can tell: — Love, the bold diver, who can cleave that still surface, and bring up into the light of heaven the rich treasures that are of Heaven's own creation.

With the four gentlemen come two ladies — young ladies, moreover, who, as penny-a-liners say, are 'possessed of considerable personal attractions.' These are the Misses Honeywood, the blooming daughters of the rector's only sister; and they have come from the far land of the North, and are looking as fresh and sweet as their own heathery hills. The roses of health that bloom upon their cheeks have been brought into full blow by the keen, sharp breeze; the shepherd's-plaid shawls drawn tightly around them give the outline of figures that gently swell into the luxuriant line of beauty and grace. Altogether, they are damsels who are pleasant to the eye, and very fair to look upon.

Since they had last visited their uncle four years had passed, and, in that time, they had shot up to womanhood, although they were not yet out of their teens. Their father was a landed proprietor living in north Northumberland; and, like other landed proprietors who live under the shade of the Cheviots, was rich in his flocks, and his herds, and his men-servants and his maid-servants, and his he-asses and his she-asses, and was quite a modern patriarch. During the past summer, the rector had taken a trip to Northumberland, in order to see his sister, and refresh himself with a clergyman's fortnight at Honeywood Hall, and he would not leave his sister and her husband until he had extracted from them a promise that they would bring down their two eldest daughters and christmas in Warwickshire. This was accordingly agreed to, and, more than that, acted upon; and little Mr. Bouncer and his sister Fanny were asked to meet them; but, to relieve the rector of a superfluity of lady guests, Miss Bouncer's quarters had been removed to the Manor Green.

It was quite an event in the history of our hero and his sisters. Four years ago, they, and

Kitty and Patty Honeywood, were mere chits, for whom dolls had not altogether lost their interest, and who considered it as promotion when they sat in the drawing-room on company evenings, instead of being shown up at dessert. Four years at this period of life makes a vast change in young ladies, and the Green and Honeywood girls had so altered since last they met, that they had almost needed a fresh introduction to each other. But a day's intimacy made them bosom friends; and the Manor Green soon saw such revels as it had not seen for many a long year.

Every night there were (in the language of the play-bills of provincial theatres) 'singing and dancing, with a variety of other entertainments;' the 'other entertainments' occasionally consisting (as is scandalously affirmed) of a very favourite class of entertainment — popular at all times, but running mad riot at the Christmas season — wherein two performers of either sex take their places beneath a white-berried bough, and go through a species of dance, or *pas de fascination*, accompanied by mysterious rites and solemnities that have been scrupulously observed, and handed down to us, from the earliest age.

Mr. Verdant Green, during the short — alas! *too* short — Christmas week, had performed more polkas than he had ever danced in his life; and, under the charming tuition of Miss Patty Honeywood, was fast becoming a proficient in the *valse a deux temps*. As yet, the whirl of the dance brought on a corresponding rotatory motion of the brain, that made everything swim before his spectacles in a way which will be easily understood by all bad travellers who have crossed from Dover to Calais with a chopping sea and a gale of wind. But Miss Patty Honeywood was both good-natured and persevering: and she allowed our hero to dance on her feet without a murmur, and watchfully guided him when his giddy vision would have led them into contact with foreign bodies.

It is an old saying, that Gratitude begets Love. Mr. Verdant Green had already reached the first part of this dangerous creation, for he felt grateful to the pretty Patty for the good-humoured trouble she bestowed on the awkwardness, which he now, for the first time, began painfully to perceive. But, what his gratitude might end in, he had perhaps never taken the trouble to inquire. It was enough to Mr. Verdant Green that he enjoyed the present; and, as to the future, he fully followed out the Horatian precept —

Quid sit futurum cras, fuge quarere;
. . . nec dulces amores
Sperne, puer, necque tuc choreas.

It was perhaps ungrateful in our hero to prefer Miss Patty Honeywood to Miss Fanny Bouncer, especially when the latter was staying in the house, and had been so warmly recommended to his notice by her vivacious brother. Especially, too, as there was nothing to be objected to in Miss Bouncer, saving the fact that some might have affirmed she was a trifle too much inclined to *embonpoint*, and was indeed a bouncer in person as well as in name. Especially, too, as Miss Fanny Bouncer was both good-humoured and clever, and, besides being mistress of the usual young-lady accomplishments, was a clever proficient in the fascinating art of photography, and had brought her camera and chemicals, and had not only calotyped Mr. Verdant Green, but had made no end of duplicates of him, in a manner that was suggestive of the deepest admiration and affection. But these sort of likings are not made to rule, and Mr. Verdant Green could see Miss Fanny Bouncer approach without betraying any of those symptoms of excitement, under the influence of which we had the privilege to see him, as he gazed from the window of his paternal mansion, and then, on beholding the approaching form of Miss Patty Honeywood, rush wildly to the vestibule.

The party had no occasion to ring, for the hall door was already opened for them, and Mr. Verdant Green was soon exchanging a delightful pressure of the hand with the blooming Patty.

'We were such a formidable party,' said that young lady, as she laughed merrily, and thereby disclosed to the enraptured gazer a remarkably even set of white teeth ('All her own, too!' as little Mr. Bouncer afterwards remarked to the enraptured gazer); 'we were such a formidable party,' said Miss Patty, 'that papa and mamma declared they would stay behind at the Rectory, and would not join in such a visitation.'

Mr. Verdant Green replies, 'Oh dear! I am very sorry,' and looks remarkably delighted — though it certainly may not be at the absence of the respected couple; and he then proclaims that everything is ready, and that Miss Bouncer and his sisters had found out some capital words.

'What a mysterious communication, Verdant!' remarks the rector, as they pass into the house. But the rector is only to be let so far into the secret as to be informed that, at the evening party which is to be held at the Manor

Green that night, a charade or two will be acted, in order to diversify the amusements. The Misses Honeywood are great adepts in this sort of pastime; so, also, are Miss Bouncer and her brother. For although the latter does not shine as a mimic, yet, as he is never deserted by his accustomed coolness, he has plenty of the *nonchalance* and readiness which is a requisite for charade acting. The Miss Honeywoods and Mr. Bouncer have therefore suggested to Mr. Verdant Green and his sisters, that to get up a little amateur performance would be 'great fun;' and the suggestion has met with a warm approval.

The drawing-room at the Manor Green opened by large folding-doors to the library; so (as Mr. Bouncer observed to our hero), 'there you've got your stage and your drop-scene as right as a trivet; and, if you stick a lot of candles and lights on each side of the doors in the library, there you'll have a regular flare-up that'll show off your venerable giglamps no end.'

So charades were determined on; and, when words had been hunted up, a council of war was called. But, as the ladies and gentlemen hold their council with closed doors, we cannot intrude upon them. We must therefore wait till the evening, when the result of their deliberations will be publicly manifested.

9

Mr. Verdant Green Makes his First Appearance on any Boards

It is the last night of December. The old year, worn out and spent with age, lies a-dying [sic], wrapped in sheets of snow.

A stern stillness reigns around. The steps of men are muffled; no echoing footfalls disturb the solemn nature of the time. The little runnels weep icy tears. The dark pines hang out their funereal plumes, and nod with their weight of snow. The elms have thrown off their green robes of joy, and, standing up in gaunt nakedness, wildly toss to heaven their imploring arms. The old year lies a-dying.

Silently through the snow steal certain carriages to the portals of the Manor Green: and, with a ringing of bells and a banging of steps, the occupants disappear in a stream of light that issues from the hall door. Mr. Green's small sanctum to the right of the hall has been converted into a cloak-room, and is fitted up with a ladies'-maid and a looking-glass, in a manner not to be remembered by the oldest inhabitant.

There the finishing stroke of ravishment is given to the toilette disarranged by a long drive through the impeding snow. There Miss Parkington (whose papa has lately revived his old school friendship with Mr. Green) discovers, to her unspeakable disgust, that the ten mile drive through the cold has invested her cheek with purple tints, and given to her *retrousse* (ill-natured people call it 'pug') nose a hue that mocks

The turkey's crested fringe.

There, too, Miss Waters (whose paternities had hitherto only been on morning-call terms with the Manor Green people, but had brushed up their acquaintance now that there was a son of marriageable years and heir to an independent fortune) discovers to her dismay that the joltings received during a six-mile drive through snowed-up lanes, have somewhat deteriorated the very full-dress aspect of her attire, and considerably flattened its former balloon-like dimensions. And there, too, Miss Brindle (whose family have been hunted up for the occasion) makes the alarming discovery that, in the lurch which their hack-fly had made at the cross roads, her brother Alfred's patent boots had not only dragged off some yards (more or less) of her flounces, but had also — to use her own mystical language — 'torn her skirt at the gathers!'

All, however, is put right as far as possible. A warm at the sanctum's fire diminishes the purple in Miss Parkington's cheeks; and the maid, by some hocus-pocus peculiar to her craft, again inflates Miss Waters into a balloon, and stitches up Miss Brindle's flounces and 'gathers.' The ladies join their respective gentlemen, who have been cooling their toes and uttering warm anathemas in the hall; and the party sail, arm-in-arm, into the drawing-room, and forthwith fall to lively remarks on that neutral ground of conversation, the weather.

Mr. Verdant Green is there, dressed with elaborate magnificence; but he continues in a state of listless apathy, and is indifferent to the 'lively' rattle of the balloon-like Miss Waters, until John the footman (who is suffering from influenza) rouses him into animation by the magic talisman 'Bister, Bissis, an' the Biss 'Oneywoods;' when he beams through his spectacles in the most benign and satisfied manner.

The Misses Honeywood are as blooming as usual: the cold air, instead of spoiling their good looks, has but improved their healthy style of beauty; and they smile, laugh, and talk in a perfectly easy, unaffected, and natural manner. Mr. Verdant Green at once makes his way to Miss Patty Honeywood's side, and, gracefully standing beside her, coffee-cup in hand, plunges headlong into the depths of a tangled conversation.

Meanwhile, the drawing-room of the Manor Green becomes filled in a way that has not been seen for many a long year; and the intelligent Mr. Mole, the gardener (who has been impressed as an odd man for the occasion, and is served up in a pseudo-livery to make him more presentable), sees more 'genteel' people than have, for a long time, been visible to his naked eye. The intelligent Mr. Mole, when he has afterwards been restored to the bosom of Mrs. Mole and his family, confides to his equally intelligent helpmate that, in his opinion, 'Master has guv the party to get husbands for the young ladies' — an opinion which, though perhaps not founded on fact so far as it related to the party which was the subject of Mr. Mole's remark, would doubtless be applicable to many similar parties given under somewhat similar circumstances.

It is not improbable that the intelligent Mr. Mole may have based his opinion on a circumstance — which, to a gentleman of his sagacity, must have carried great weight — namely, that whenever in the course of the evening the hall was made the promenade for the loungers and dancers, he perceived, firstly, that Miss Green was invariably accompanied by Mr. Charles Larkyns; secondly, that the Rev. Josiah Meek kept Miss Helen dallying about the wine and lemonade tray much longer than was necessary for the mere consumption of the cooling liquids; and thirdly, that Miss Fanny, who was a pert, talkative Miss of sixteen, was continually to be found there with either Mr. Henry Bouncer or Mr. Alfred Brindle dancing attendance upon her. But, be this as it may, the intelligent Mr. Mole was impressed with the conviction that Mr. Green had called his young friends together as to a matrimonial auction, and that his daughters were to be put up without reserve, and knocked down to the highest bidder.

All the party have arrived. The weather has been talked over for the last time (for the present); a harp, violin, and a cornet-a-piston from the county town, influenced by the spirit of gin-and-water, are heard discoursing most eloquent music in the dining-room, which has been cleared out for the dance. Miss Patty Honeywood, accepting the offer of Mr. Verdant Green's arm, swims joyously out of the room; other ladies and gentlemen pair, and follow: the ball is opened.

A polka follows the quadrille; and, while the dancers rest awhile from their exertions, or crowd around the piano in the drawing-room to hear the balloon-like Miss Waters play a firework piece of music, in which execution takes the place of melody, and chromatic scales are discharged from her fingers like showers of rockets, Mr. Verdant Green mysteriously weeds out certain members of the party, and vanishes with them up-stairs.

When Miss Waters has discharged all her fireworks, and has descended from the throne of her music-stool, a set of Lancers is formed; and, while the usual mistakes are being made in the figures, the dancers find a fruitful subject of conversation in surmises that a charade is going to be acted. The surmise proves to be correct; for when the set has been brought to an end with that peculiar in-and-out tum-tum-tiddle-iddle-tum-tum-tum movement which characterizes the last figure of *Les Lanciers*, the trippers on the light fantastic toe are requested to assemble in the drawing-room, where the chairs and couches have been pulled up to face the folding doors that lead into the library. Mr. Verdant Green appears; and, after announcing that the word to be acted will be one of three syllables, and that each syllable will be represented by itself, and that then the complete word will be given, throws open the folding doors for

SCENE I. *Syllable* 1. — Enter the Miss Honeywoods, dressed in fashionable bonnets and shawls. They are shown in by a footman (Mr. Bouncer) attired in a peculiarly ingenious and effective livery, made by pulling up the trousers to the knee, and wearing the dress-coat inside out, so as to display the crimson silk linings of the sleeves: the effect of Mr. Bouncer's appearance is considerably heightened by a judicious outlay of flour sprinkled over his hair. Mr. Bouncer (as footman) gives the ladies chairs, and inquires, 'What name shall I be pleased to say, mem?' Miss Patty answers in a languid and fashionable voice, 'The Ladies Louisa and Arabella Mountfidget.' Mr. Bouncer evaporates with a low bow, leaving the ladies to play with their parasols, and converse. Lady Arabella (Miss Patty) then expresses a devout wish that Lady Trotter (wife of Sir Lambkin Trotter, Bart.), in whose house they are supposed to be, will not keep them waiting as long as she detained her aunt, Lady Bellwether, when the poor old lady fell asleep from sheer fatigue, and was found snoring on the sofa. Lady Louisa then falls to an inspection of the card-tray, and reads the paste-boards of some high-sounding titles not to be found in Debrett, and expresses wonder as to where Lady Trotter can have picked up the Duchess of Ditchwater's card, as she (Lady Louisa) is morally convinced that her Grace can never have condescended to have even sent in her card by a footman. Becoming impatient at the non-appearance of Lady Trotter, Miss Patty Honeywood then rings the bell, and, with much asperity of manner, inquires of Mr. Bouncer (as footman) if Lady Trotter is informed that the Ladies Louisa and Arabella Mountfidget are waiting to see her? Mr. Bouncer replies, with a footman's bow, and a footman's *h*exasperation of his h's, 'Me lady is haweer hof your ladyships' visit; but me lady is at present hunable to happear: me lady, 'owever, has give me a message, which she hasks me to deliver to your ladyships.' 'Then why don't you deliver it at once,' says Miss Patty, 'and not waste the valuable time of the Ladies Louisa and Arabella Mountfidget? What *is* the message?' 'Me lady,' replies Mr. Bouncer, 'requests me to present her compliments to your ladyships, and begs me to hinform you that me lady is a cleaning of herself!' Amid great laughter from the audience, the Ladies Mountfidget toss their heads and flutter grandly out of the room, followed by the floured footman; while Mr. Verdant Green, unseen by those in front, pushes-to the folding doors, to show that the first syllable is performed.

Praises of the acting, and guesses at the word, agreeably fill up the time till the next scene. The Rev. Josiah Meek, who is not much used to charades, confides to Miss Helen Green that he surmises the word to be, either 'visitor' or 'impudence;' but, as the only ground to this surmise rests on these two words being words of three syllables, Miss Helen gently repels the idea, and sagely observes, 'we shall see more in the next scene.'

SCENE II. *Syllable 2.* — The folding-doors open, and discover Mr. Verdant Green, as a sick gentleman, lying on a sofa, in a dressing-gown, with pillows under his head, and Miss Patty Honeywood in attendance upon him. A table, covered with glasses and medicine bottles, is drawn up to the sufferer's couch in an inviting manner. Miss Patty informs the sufferer that the time is come for him to take his draught. The sufferer groans in a dismal manner, and says, 'Oh! is it, my dear?' She replies, 'Yes! you must take it now;' and sternly pours some sherry wine out of the medicine bottle into a cup. The sufferer makes piteous faces, and exclaims, 'It is so nasty, I can't take it, my love!' (It is to be observed that Mr. Verdant Green, skilfully taking advantage of the circumstance that Miss Patty Honeywood is supposed to represent the wife of the sufferer, plentifully besprinkles his conversation with endearing epithets.) When, after much persuasion and groaning, the sufferer has been induced to take his medicine, his spouse announces the arrival of the doctor; when, enter Mr. Bouncer, still floured as to his head, but wearing spectacles, a long black coat, and a shirt-frill, and having his dress otherwise altered so as to represent a medical man of the old school. The doctor asks what sort of a night his patient has had, inspects his tongue with professional gravity, feels his pulse, looks at his watch, and mysteriously shakes his head. He then commences thrusting and poking Mr. Verdant Green in various parts of his body, — after the manner of doctors with their victims, and farmers with their beasts, — inquiring between each poke, 'Does that hurt you?' and being answered by a convulsive 'Oh!' and a groan of agony. The doctor then prescribes a draught to be taken every half-hour, with the pills and blister at bed-time; and, after covering his two fellow-actors with confusion, by observing that he leaves his patient in admirable hands, and, that in an affection of the heart, the application of lip-salve and warm treatment will give a decided tone to the system, and produce soothing and grateful emotions — takes his leave; and the folding-doors are closed on the blushes of Miss Patty Honeywood, and Mr. Verdant Green.

More applause: more agreeable conversation: more ingenious speculations. The Rev. Josiah Meek is now of opinion that the word is either 'medicine' or 'suffering.' Miss Helen still sagely observes, 'we shall see more in the next scene.'

SCENE III. *Syllable 3.* — Mr. Verdant Green discovered sitting at a table furnished with pens and ink, books, and rolls of paper. Mr. Verdant Green wears on his head a Chelsea pensioner's cocked-hat (the 'property' of the Family, — as Mr. Footelights would have said), folded into a shovel shape; and is supposed to accurately represent the outside of a London publisher. To him enter Mr. Bouncer — the flour off his head — coat buttoned tightly to the throat, no visible linen, and wearing in his face and appearance generally, 'the garb of humility.' Says the publisher 'Now, sir, please to state your business, and be quick about it: I am much engaged in looking over for the press a work of a distinguished author, which I am just about to publish.' Meekly replies the other, as he holds under his arm an immense paper packet: 'It is about a work of my own, sir, that I have now ventured to intrude upon you. I have here, sir, a small manuscript,' (producing his roll of a book), 'which I am ambitious to see given to the world through the medium of your printing establishment.' To him, the Publisher — 'Already am I inundated with manuscripts on all possible subjects, and cannot undertake to look at any more for some time to come. What is the nature of your manuscript?' Meekly replies the other — 'The theme of my work, sir, is a History of England before the Flood. The subject is both new and interesting. It is to be presumed that our beloved country existed before the Flood: if so, it must have had a history. I have therefore endeavoured to fill up what is lacking in the annals of our land, by a record of its antediluvian state, adapted to the meanest comprehension, and founded on the most baseless facts. I am desirous, sir, to see myself in print. I should like my work, sir, to appear in large letters; in very large letters, sir. Indeed, sir, it would give me joy, if you would condescend to print it altogether in capital letters: my *magnum opus* might then be called with truth, a capital work.' To him, the Publisher — 'Much certainly depends on the character of the printing.' Meekly the author — 'Indeed, sir, it does. A great book, sir, should be printed in great letters. If you will permit me, I will show you the size of the letters in which I should wish my book to be printed.' Mr. Bouncer then points out in some books on the table, the printing he most admires; and, beseeching the Publisher to read over his manuscript, and think favourably of his History of England before the Flood, makes his bow to Mr. Verdant Green and the Chelsea pensioner's cocked hat.

More applause, and speculations. The Rev. Josiah Meek confident that he has discovered the word. It must be either 'publisher' or 'authorship.' Miss Helen still sage.

SCENE IV. *The Word*. — Miss Bouncer discovered with her camera, arranging her photographic chemicals. She soliloquizes: 'There! now, all is ready for my sitter.' She calls the footman (Mr. Verdant Green), and says, 'John, you may show the Lady Fitz-Canute upstairs.' The footman shows in Miss Honeywood, dressed in an antiquated bonnet and mantle, waving a huge fan. John gives her a chair, into which she drops, exclaiming, 'What an insufferable toil it is to ascend to these elevated Photographic rooms;' and makes good use of her fan. Miss Bouncer then fixes the focus of her camera, and begs the Lady Fitz-Canute to sit perfectly still, and to call up an agreeable smile to her face. Miss Honeywood thereupon disposes her face in ludicrous 'wreathed smiles;' and Miss Bouncer's head disappears under the velvet hood of the camera. 'I am afraid,' at length says Miss Bouncer, 'I am afraid that I shall not be able to succeed in taking a likeness of your ladyship this morning.' 'And why, pray?' asks her ladyship with haughty surprise. 'Because it is a gloomy day,' replies the Photographer, 'and much depends upon the rays of light.' 'Then procure the rays of light!' 'That is more than I can do.' 'Indeed! I suppose if the Lady Fitz-Canute wishes for the rays of light, and condescends to pay for the rays of light, she can obtain the rays of light.' Miss Bouncer considers this too *exigeant*, and puts her sitter off by promising to complete a most fascinating portrait of her on some more favourable day. Lady Fitz-Canute appears to be somewhat mollified at this, and is graciously pleased to observe, 'Then I will undergo the fatigue of ascending to these elevated Photographic rooms at some future period. But, mind, when I next come, that you procure the rays of light!' So she is shown out by Mr. Verdant Green, and the folding-doors are closed amid applause, and the audience distract themselves with guesses as to the word.

'Photograph' is a general favourite, but is found not to agree with the three first scenes, although much ingenuity is expended in endeavouring to make them fit the word. The Curate makes a headlong rush at the word 'Daguerreotype,' and is confident that he has solved the problem, until he is informed that it is a word of more than three syllables. Charles Larkyns has already whispered the word to Mary Green; but they keep their discovery to themselves. At length, the Rev. Josiah Meek, in a moment of inspiration, hits upon the word, and proclaims it to be CALOTYPE ('Call — oh! — type;') upon which Mr. Alfred Brindle declares to Miss Fanny Green that he had fancied it must be that, all along, and, in fact, was just on the point of saying it: and the actors, coming in in a body, receive the violet-crowns and laurel-wreaths of praise as the meed of their exertions. Perhaps, the Miss Honeywoods and Mr. Bouncer receive larger crowns than the others, but Mr. Verdant Green gets his due share, and is fully satisfied with his first appearance on 'the boards.'

Dancing then succeeds, varied by songs from the young ladies, and discharges of chromatic fireworks from the fingers of Miss Waters, for whom Charles Larkyns does the polite, in turning over the leaves of her music. Then some carol-singers come to the Hall-door, and the bells of the church proclaim, in joyful peals, the birth of the New Year; — a new year of hopes, and joys, and cares, and griefs, and unions, and partings; — a new year of which, who then present shall see the end? who shall be there to welcome in its successor? who shall be absent, laid in the secret places of the earth? Ah, *who*? For, even in the midst of revelry and youth, the joy-peals of those old church bells can strike the key-note of a wail of grief.

Another charade follows, in which new actors join. Then comes a merry supper, in which Mr. Alfred Brindle, in order to give himself courage to appear in the next charade, takes more champagne than is good for him; in which, too (probably, from similar champagney reasons), Miss Parkington's unfortunately self-willed nose again assumes a more roseate hue than is becoming to a maiden; in which, too, Mr. Verdant Green being called upon to return thanks for 'the ladies' — (toast, proposed in eloquent terms by H. Bouncer, Esq., and drunk 'with the usual honours,') — is so alarmed at finding himself upon his legs, that his ideas altogether vanish, and in great confusion of utterance, he observes, — 'I-I-ladies and gentleman-feel-I-I-a-feel-assure you-grattered and flattified-I mean, flattered and gratified-being called on-return thanks-I-I-a-the ladies-give a larm to chife — I mean, charm to life — (*applause*)-and-a-a-grace by their table this presence, -I mean-a-a- (*applause*) — and joytened our eye-I mean, heighted our joy, to-night- (*applause*) — in their name-thanks-honour.' Mr. Verdant Green takes advantage of the applause which follows these incoherent remarks, and sits down, covered with confusion, but thankful that the struggle is over.

More dancing follows. Our hero performs prodigies in the *valse a deux temps*, and twirls about until he has not a leg left to stand upon. The harp, the violin, and the cornet-a-piston, from the county town, play mechanically in their sleep, and can only be roused by repeated applications of gin-and-water. Carriages are ordered round: wraps are in requisition: the mysterious rites under the white-berried bush are stealthily repeated for the last time: the guests depart, as it were, in a heap; the Rectory party being the last to leave. The intelligent Mr. Mole, who has fuddled himself by an injudicious mixture of the half-glasses of wine left on the supper-table, is exasperated with the butler for not allowing him to assist in putting away the silver; and declares that he (the butler) is 'a hold himage,' for which, he (the intelligent Mr. M.), 'don't care a button!' and, as the epithet 'image' appears to wondrously offend the butler, Mr. Mole is removed from further consequences by his intelligent wife, who is waiting to conduct her lord and master home.

At length, the last light is out in the Manor Green. Mr. Verdant Green is lying uncomfortably upon his back, and is waltzing through Dreamland with the blooming Patty Honeywood.

10

Mr. Verdant Green Enjoys a Real Cigar

The Christmas vacation passed rapidly away; the Honeywood family returned to the far north; and, once more, Mr. Verdant Green found himself within the walls of Brazenface. He and Mr. Bouncer had together gone up to Oxford, leaving Charles Larkyns behind to keep a grace-term.

Charles Larkyns had determined to take a good degree. For some time past, he had been reading steadily; and, though only a few hours in each day may be given to books — yet, when that is done, with regularity and painstaking, a real and sensible progress is made. He knew that he had good abilities, and he had determined not to let them remain idle any longer, but to make that use of them for which they were given to him. His examination would come on during the next term; and he hoped to turn the interval to good account, and be able in the end to take a respectable degree. He was destined for the Bar; and, as he had no wish to be a briefless

Barrister, he knew that college honours would be of great advantage to him in his after career. He, at once, therefore, set bodily to work to read up his subjects; while his father assisted him in his labours, and Mary Green smiled a kind approval.

Meanwhile, his friends, Mr. Verdant Green and Mr. Henry Bouncer, were enjoying Oxford life, and disporting themselves among the crowd of skaters in the Christ Church meadows. And a very different scene did the meadows present to the time when they had last skimmed over its surface. Then, the green fields were covered with Sailing-boats, out-riggers, and punts, and Mr. Verdant Green had nearly come to an untimely end in the waters. But now the scene was changed! Jack Frost had stepped in, and had seized the flood in his frozen fingers, and had bound it up in an icy breast-plate.

And a capital place did the meadows make for any Undergraduate who was either a professed skater, or whose skating education (as in the case of our hero) had been altogether neglected. For the water was only of a moderate depth; so that, in the event of the ice giving way, there was nothing to fear beyond a slight and partial ducking. This was especially fortunate for Mr. Verdant Green, who, after having experienced total submersion and a narrow escape from drowning on that very spot, would never have been induced to again commit himself to the surface of the deep, had he not been fully convinced that the deep had now subsided into a shallow. With his breast fortified by this resolution, he therefore fell a victim to the syren tongue of Mr. Bouncer, when that gentleman observed to him with sincere feeling, 'Giglamps, old fellow! it would be a beastly shame, when there's such jolly ice, if you did not learn to skate; especially, as I can show you the trick.'

For, Mr. Bouncer was not only skilful with his hands and arms, but could also perform feats with his feet. He could not only dance quadrilles in dress boots in a ball-room, but he could also go through the figures on the ice in a pair of skates. He could do the outside edge at a more acute angle than the generality of people; he could cut figures of eight that were worthy of Cocker himself, he could display spread-eagles that would have astonished the Fellows of the Zoological Society. He could skim over the thinnest ice in the most don't-care way; and, when at full speed, would stoop to pick up a stone. He would take a hop-skip-and-a-jump; and would vault over walking-sticks, as easily as if he were on dry land, — an accomplishment which he had learnt of the Count Doembrownski, a Russian gentleman, who, in his own country, lived chiefly on skates, and, in this country, on pigeons, and whose short residence in Oxford was suddenly brought to a full stop by the arbitrary power of the Vice-Chancellor. So, Mr. Verdant Green was persuaded to purchase, and put on a pair of skates, and to make his first appearance as a skater in the Christ Church meadows, under the auspices of Mr. Bouncer.

The sensation of first finding yourself in a pair of skates is peculiar. It is not unlike the sensation which must have been felt by the young bear, when he was dropped from his mamma's mouth, and, for the first time, told to walk. The poor little bear felt, that it was all very well to say 'walk,' — but how was he to do it? Was he to walk with his right fore-leg only? or, with his left fore-leg? or, with both his fore-legs? or, was he to walk with his right hind-leg? or, with his left hind-leg? or, with both his hind-legs? or, was he to make a combination of hind and fore-legs, and walk with all four at once? or, what was he to do? So he tried each of these ways; and they all failed. Poor little bear!

Mr. Verdant Green felt very much in the little bear's condition. He was undecided whether to skate with his right leg, or with his left leg, or with both his legs. He tried his right leg, and immediately it glided off at right angles with his body, while his left leg performed a similar and spontaneous movement in the contrary direction. Having captured his left leg, he put it cautiously forwards, and immediately it twisted under him, while his right leg amused itself by describing an altogether unnecessary circle. Obtaining a brief mastery over both legs, he put them forwards at the same moment, and they fled from beneath him, and he was flung — bump! — on his back. Poor little bear!

But, if it is hard to make a start in a pair of skates when you are in a perpendicular position, how much is the difficulty increased when your position has become a horizontal one! You raise yourself on your knees, — you assist yourself with your hands, — and, no sooner have you got one leg right, than away slides the other, and down you go. It is like the movement in that scene with the pair of short stilts, in which the French clowns are so amusing, and it is almost as difficult to perform. Mr. Verdant Green soon found that though he might be ambitious to excel in the polite accomplishment of skating, yet that his ambition was destined to meet with many a fall. But he persevered, and perseverance will achieve wonders, especially when aided by the tuition of such an indefatigable gentleman as Mr. Bouncer.

'You get on stunningly, Giglamps,' said the little gentleman, 'and haven't been on your beam ends more than once a minute. But I should advise you, old fellow, to get your sit-upons seated with wash-leather, — just like the eleventh hussars do with their cherry-coloured pants. It'll come cheaper in the end, and may be productive of comfort. And now, after all these exciting ups and downs, let us go and have a quiet hand at billiards.' So the two friends strolled up the High, where they saw two Queensmen 'confessing their shame,' as Mr. Bouncer phrased it, by standing under the gateway of their college; and went on to Bickerton's, where they found all the tables occupied, and Jonathan playing a match with Mr. Fluke of Christ Church. So, after watching the celebrated marker long enough to inspire them with a desire to accomplish similar feats of dexterity, they continued their walk to Broad Street, and, turning up a yard opposite to the Clarendon, found that Betteris had an upstair room at liberty. Here they accomplished several pleasing mathematical problems with the balls, and contributed their modicum towards the smoking of the ceiling of the room.

Since Mr. Verdant Green had acquired the art of getting through a cigar without making himself ill, he had looked upon himself as a genuine smoker; and had, from time to time, bragged of his powers as regarded the fumigation of 'the herb Nicotiana, commonly called tobacco,' (as the Oxford statute tersely says). This was an amiable weakness on his part that had not escaped the observant eye of Mr. Bouncer, who had frequently taken occasion, in the presence of his friends, to defer to Mr. Verdant Green's judgment in the matter of cigars. The train of adulation being thus laid, an opportunity was only needed to fire it. It soon came.

'Once upon a time,' as the story-books say, it chanced that Mr. Bouncer was consuming his minutes and cigars at his tobacconist's, when his eye lighted for the thousandth time on the roll of cabbage-leaves, brown paper, and refuse tobacco, which being done up into the form of a monster cigar (a foot long, and of proportionate thickness), was hung in the shop window, and did duty as a truthful token of the commodity vended within. Mr. Bouncer had looked at this implement nine hundred and ninety-nine times, without its suggesting anything else to his mind, than its being of the same class of art as the monster mis-representations outside wild-beast shows;

but he now gazed upon it with new sensations. In short, Mr. Bouncer took such a fancy to the thing, that he purchased it, and took it off to his rooms, — though he did not mention this fact to his friend, Mr. Verdant Green, when he saw him soon afterwards, and spoke to him of his excellent judgment in tobacco.

'A taste for smoke comes natural, Giglamps!' said Mr. Bouncer. 'It's what you call a *nascitur non fit*; and, if you haven't the gift, why you can't purchase it. Now, you're a judge of smoke; it's a gift with you, don't you see; and you could no more help knowing a good weed from a bad one, than you could help waggling your tail if you were a baa-lamb.'

Mr. Verdant Green bowed, and blushed, in acknowledgment of this delightful flattery.

'Now, there's old Footelights, you know; he's got an uncle, who's a governor, or some great swell, out in Barbadoes. Well, every now and then the old trump sends Footelights no end of a box of weeds; not common ones, you understand, but regular tip-toppers; but they're quite thrown away on poor Footelights, who'd think as much of cabbage-leaves as he would of real Havannahs, so he's always obliged to ask somebody else's opinion about them. Well, he's got a sample of a weed of a most terrific kind: — *Magnifico Pomposo* is the name;

— no end uncommon, and at least a foot long. We don't meet with 'em in England because they're too expensive to import. Well, it wouldn't do to throw away such a weed as this on any one; so, Footelights wants to have the opinion of a man who's really a judge of what a good weed is. I refused, because my taste has been rather out of order lately; and Billy Blades is in training for Henley, so he's obliged to decline; so I told him of you, Giglamps, and said, that if there was a man in Brazenface that could tell him what his Magnifico Pomposo was worth, that man was Verdant Green. Don't blush, old feller! you can't help having a fine judgment, you know; so don't be ashamed of it. Now, you must wine with me this evening; Footelights and some more men are coming; and we're all anxious to hear your opinion about these new weeds, because, if it's favourable we can club together, and import a box.' Mr. Bouncer's victim, being perfectly unconscious of the trap laid for him, promised to come to the wine, and give his opinion on this weed of fabled size and merit.

When the evening and company had come, he was rather staggered at beholding the dimensions of the pseudo-cigar; but, rashly judging that to express surprise would be to betray ignorance, Mr. Verdant Green inspected the formidable monster with the air of a connoisseur, and smelt, pinched, and rolled his tongue round it, after the manner of the best critics. If this was a diverting spectacle to the assembled guests of Mr. Bouncer, how must the humour of the scene have been increased, when our hero, with great difficulty, lighted the cigar, and, with still greater difficulty, held it in his mouth, and endeavoured to smoke it! As Mr. Foote afterwards observed, 'it was a situation for a screaming farce.'

'It doesn't draw well!' faltered the victim, as the bundle of rubbish went out for the fourth time.

'Why, that's always the case with the Barbadoes baccy!' said Mr. Bouncer; 'it takes a long pull, and a strong pull, and a pull all together to get it to make a start; but when once it does go, it goes beautiful — like a house a-fire. But you can't expect it to be like a common threepenny weed. Here! let me light him for you, Giglamps; I'll give the beggar a dig in his ribs, as a gentle persuader.' Mr. Bouncer thereupon poked his penknife through the rubbish, and after a time induced it to 'draw'; and Mr. Verdant Green pulled at it furiously, and made his eyes water with the unusual cloud of smoke that he raised.

'And now, what d'ye think of it, my

beauty?' inquired Mr. Bouncer. 'It's something out of the common, ain't it?'

'It has a beautiful ash!' observed Mr. Smalls.

'And diffuses an aroma that makes me long to defy the trainer, and smoke one like it!' said Mr. Blades.

'So pray give me your reading — at least, your opinion, — on my Magnifico Pomposo!' asked Mr. Foote.

'Well,' answered Mr. Verdant Green, slowly — turning very pale as he spoke, — 'at first, I thought it was be-yew-tiful; but, altogether, I think-that-the Barbadoes tobacco-doesn't quite-agree with-my stom-' the speaker abruptly concluded, by dropping the cigar, putting his handkerchief to his mouth, and rushing into Mr. Bouncer's bedroom. The Magnifico Pomposo had been too much for him, and had produced sensations accurately interpreted by Mr. Bouncer, who forthwith represented in expressive pantomime, the actions of a distressed voyager, when he feebly murmurs 'Steward!'

To atone for the 'chaffing' which he had been the means of inflicting on his friend, the little gentleman, a few days afterwards, proposed to take our hero to the Chipping Norton Steeple-chase, — Mr. Smalls and Mr. Fosbrooke making up the quartet for a tandem. It was on their return from the races, that, after having stopped at *The Bear* at Woodstock, 'to wash out the horses' mouths,' and having done this so effectually that the horses had appeared to have no mouths left, and had refused to answer the reins, and had smashed the cart against a house, which had seemed to have danced into the middle of the road for their diversion, — and, after having put back to *The Bear*, and prevailed upon that animal to lend them a nondescript vehicle of the 'pre-adamite buggy' species, described by Sidney Smith, — that, much time having been consumed by the progress of this chapter of accidents, they did not reach Peyman's Gate until a late hour; and Mr. Verdant Green found that he was once more in difficulties. For they had no sooner got through the gate, than the wild octaves from Mr. Bouncer's post-horn were suddenly brought to a full stop, and Mr. Fosbrooke, who was the 'waggoner,' was brought to Woh! and was compelled to pull up in obedience to the command of the proctor, who, as on a previous occasion, suddenly appeared from behind the toll-house, in company with his marshal and bull-dogs.

The Sentence pronounced on our hero the next day, was, 'Sir! — You will translate all your lectures; have your name crossed on the buttery and kitchen books; and be confined to chapel, hall, and college.'

This sentence was chiefly annoying, inasmuch as it somewhat interfered with the duties and pleasures attendant upon his boating practice. For, wonderful to relate, Mr. Verdant Green had so much improved in the science, that he was now 'Number 3' of his college 'Torpid,' and was in hard training. The Torpid races commenced on March 10th, and were continued on the following days. Our hero sent his father a copy of *Tintinnabulum's Life*, which — after informing the Manor Green family that 'the boats took up positions in the following order: 'Brazenose, Exeter I, Wadham, Balliol, St. John's, Pembroke, University, Oriel, Brazenface, Christ Church I, Worcester, Jesus, Queen's, Christ Church 2, Exeter 2' — proceeded to enter into particulars of each day's sport, of which it is only necessary to record such as gave interest to our hero's family.

'First day*** Brazenface refused to acknowledge the bump by Christ Church (I) before they came to the Cherwell. There is very little doubt but that they were bumped at the Gut and the Willows . . .

'Second day*** Brazenface rowed pluckily away from Worcester . . .

'Third day*** A splendid race between Brazenface and Worcester; and, at the flag, the latter were within a foot; they did not, however, succeed in bumping. The cheering from the Brazenface barge was vociferous . . .

'Fourth day*** Worcester was more fortunate, and succeeded in making the bump at the Cherwell, in consequence of No. 3 of the Brazenface boat fainting from fatigue.'

Under 'No. 3' Mr. Verdant Green had drawn a pencil line, and had written 'V.G.' He shortly after related to his family the gloomy particulars of the bump, when he returned home for the Easter vacation.

11

Mr. Verdant Green Gets Through his Smalls

Despite the hindrance which the *grande passion* is supposed to bring to the student, Charles Larkyns had made very good use of the opportunities afforded him by the leisure of his grace-term. Indeed, as he himself observed,

'Who hath not owned, with rapture-
smitten frame,
The power of *grace!*'

And as he felt that the hours of his grace-term had not been wasted in idleness, but had been turned to profitable account, it is not at all unlikely that his pleasures of hope regarding his Degree-examination, and the position his name would occupy in the Class-list, were of a roseate hue. He, therefore, when the Easter vacation had come to an end, returned to Oxford in high spirits, with our hero and his friend Mr. Bouncer, who, after a brief visit to 'the Mum,' had passed the remainder of the vacation at the Manor Green. During these few holiday weeks, Charles Larkyns had acted as private tutor to his two friends, and had, in the language of Mr. Bouncer, 'put them through their paces uncommon;' for the little gentleman was going in for his Degree, *alias* Great-go, *alias* Greats; and our hero for his first examination *in literis humanioribus*, *alias* Responsions, *alias* Little-go, *alias* Smalls. Thus the friends returned to Oxford mutually benefited; but, as the time for examination drew nearer and still nearer, the fears of Mr. Bouncer rose in a gradation of terrors, that threatened to culminate in an actual panic.

'You see,' said the little gentleman, 'the Mum's set her heart on my getting through, and I must read like the doose. And I haven't got the head, you see, for Latin and Greek; and that beastly Euclid altogether stumps me; and I feel as though I should come to grief. I'm blowed,' the little gentleman would cry, earnestly and sadly, 'I'm blow'd if I don't think they must have given me too much pap when I was a babby, and softened my brains! or else, why can't I walk into these classical parties just as easy as you, Charley, or old Giglamps there? But I can't, you see: my brains are addled. They say it ain't a bad thing for reading to get your head shaved. It cools your brains, and gives full play to what you call your intellectual faculties. I think I shall try the dodge, and get a gent's real head of hair, till after the exam.; and then, when I've stumped the examiners, I can wear my own luxuriant locks again.'

And, as Mr. Bouncer professed, so did he; and, not many days after, astonished his friends and the University generally by appearing in a wig of curly black hair. It was a pleasing sight to see the little gentleman with a scalp like a billiard ball, a pipe in his mouth, and the wig mounted on a block, with books spread before him, endeavouring to persuade himself that he was working up his subjects. It was still more pleasing to view him, in moments of hilarity, divest himself of his wig, and hurl it at the scout, or any other offensive object that appeared before him. And it was a sight not to be forgotten by the beholders, when, after too recklessly partaking of an indiscriminate mixture of egg-flip, sangaree, and cider-cup, he feebly threw his wig at the spectacles of Mr. Verdant Green, and, overbalanced by the exertion, fell back into the coal-scuttle, where he lay, bald-headed and helpless, laughing and weeping by turns, and caressed by Huz and Buz.

But the shaving of his head was not the only feature (or, rather, loss of feature) that distinguished Mr. Bouncer's reading for his degree. The gentleman with the limited knowledge of the cornet-a-piston, who had the rooms immediately beneath those of our hero and his friend, had made such slow progress in his musical education, that he had even now scarcely got into his 'Cottage near a Wood.' This gentleman was Mr. Bouncer's Frankenstein. He was always rising up when he was not wanted. When Mr. Bouncer felt as if he could read, and sat down to his books, wigless and determined, the doleful legend of the cottage near a wood was forced upon him in an unpleasingly obtrusive and distracting manner. It was in vain that Mr. Bouncer sounded his octaves in all their discordant variations; the gentleman had no ear, and was not to be put out of his cottage on any terms: Mr. Bouncer's notices of ejectment were always disregarded. He had hoped that the ears of Mr. Slowcoach (whose rooms were in the angle of the Quad) would have been pierced by the noise, and that he would have put a stop to the nuisance; but, either from its being too customary a custom, or that the ears of Mr. Slowcoach had grown callous, the nuisance was suffered to continue unreproved.

Mr. Bouncer resolved, therefore, on some desperate method of calling attention to one nuisance, by creating another of a louder description; and, as his octaves appeared to fail in this, — notwithstanding the energy and annoying ability that he threw into them, — he conceived the idea of setting up a drum! The plan was no sooner thought of than carried out. He met with an instrument sufficiently large and formidable for his purpose, — hired it, and had it stealthily conveyed into college (like another Falstaff) in a linen 'buck-basket.' He waited his opportunity; and, the next time that the gentleman in the rooms beneath took his cornet to his cottage near a wood, Mr. Bouncer, stationed on the landing above, played a thundering accompaniment on his big drum.

The echoes from the tightened parchment rolled round the Quad, and brought to the spot a rush of curious and excited undergraduates. Mr. Bouncer, — after taking off his wig in honour of the air, — then treated them to the National Anthem, arranged as a drum solo for two sticks, the chorus being sustained by the voices of those present; when in the midst of the entertainment, the reproachful features of Mr. Slowcoach appeared upon the scene. Sternly the tutor demanded the reason of the strange hubbub; and was answered by Mr. Bouncer, that, as one gentleman was allowed to play *his* favourite instrument whenever he chose for his own but no one else's gratification, he could not see why he (Mr. Bouncer) might not also, whenever he pleased, play for *his* own gratification his favourite instrument — the big drum. This specious excuse, although logical, was not altogether satisfactory to Mr. Slowcoach; and, with some asperity, he ordered Mr. Bouncer never again to indulge in, what he termed (in reference probably to the little gentleman's bald head), 'such an indecent exhibition.' But, as he further ordered that the cornet-a-piston gentleman was to instrumentally enter into his cottage near a wood, only at stated hours in the afternoon, Mr. Bouncer had gained his point in putting a stop to the nuisance so far as it interfered with his reading; and, thenceforth, he might be seen on brief occasions persuading himself that he was furiously reading and getting up his subjects by the aid of those royal roads to knowledge, variously known as cribs, crams, plugs, abstracts, analyses, or epitomes.

But, besides the assistance thus afforded to him *out* of the schools, Mr. Bouncer, like many others, idle as well as ignorant, intended to assist himself when *in* the schools by any contrivance that his ingenuity could suggest, or his audacity carry out.

'It's quite fair,' was the little gentleman's argument, 'to do the examiners in any way that you can, as long as you only go in for a pass. Of course, if you were going in for a class, or a scholarship, or anything of that sort, it would be no end mean and dirty to crib; and the gent that did it ought to be kicked out of the society of gentlemen. But when you only go in for a pass, and ain't doing any one any harm by a little bit of cribbing, but choose to run the risk to save yourself the bother of being ploughed, why then, I think, a feller's bound to do what he can for himself. And, you see, in my case, Giglamps, there's the Mum to be considered; she'd cut up doosid, if I didn't get through; so I must crib a bit, if it's only for *her* sake.'

But although the little gentleman thus made filial tenderness the excuse for his deceit, and the salve for his conscience, yet he could neither persuade Mr. Verdant Green to follow his example, nor to be a convert to his opinions; nor would he be persuaded by our hero to relinquish his designs.

'Why, look here, Giglamps!' Mr. Bouncer would say; 'how *can* I relinquish them, after having had all this trouble? I'll put you up to a few of my dodges — free, gratis, for nothing. In the first place, Giglamps, you see here's a small circular bit of paper, covered with Peloponnesian and Punic wars, and no end of dates, — written small and short, you see, but quite legible, — with the chief things done in red ink. Well, this gentleman goes in the front of my watch, under the glass; and, when I get stumped for a date, out comes the watch; — I look at the time of day — you understand, and down goes the date. Here's another dodge!' added the little gentleman — who might well have been called 'the Artful Dodger' — as he produced a shirt from a drawer. 'Look here, at the wristbands! Here are all the Kings of Israel and Judah, with their dates and prophets, written down in India-ink, so as to wash out again. You twitch up the cuff of your coat, quite accidentally, and then you book your king. You see, Giglamps, I don't like to trust, as some fellows do, to having what you want, written down small and shoved into a quill, and passed to you by some man sitting in the schools; that's dangerous, don't you see. And I don't like to hold cards in my hand; I've improved on that, and invented a first-rate dodge of my own, that I intend to take out a patent for. Like all truly great inventions, it's no end simple. In the first place, look straight afore you, my little dear, and you will see this pack of cards, — all made of a size, nice to hold in the palm of your hand; they're about all sorts of rum things, — everything that I want. And you see that each beggar's got a hole drilled in him. And you see, here's a longish string with a little bit of hooked wire at the end, made so that I can easily hang the card on it. Well, I pass the string up my coat sleeve, and down under my waistcoat; and here, you see, I've got the wire end in the palm of my hand. Then, I slip out the card I want, and hook it on to the wire, so that I can have it just before me as I write. Then, if any of the examiners look suspicious, or if one of them comes round to spy, I just pull the bit of string that hangs under the bottom of my waistcoat, and away flies the card up my coat sleeve; and when the examiner comes round, he sees that my hand's never moved, and that there's nothing in it! So he walks off satisfied; and then I shake the little beggar out of my sleeve again, and the same game goes on as before. And when the string's tight, even straightening your body is quite sufficient to hoist the card into your sleeve, without moving either of your hands. I've got an Examination-coat made on purpose, with a heap of pockets, in which I can stow my cards in regular order. These three pockets,' said Mr. Bouncer, as he produced the coat, 'are entirely for Euclid. Here's each problem written right out on a card; they're laid regularly in order, and I turn them over in my pocket, till I get hold of the one I want, and then I take it out, and work it. So you see, Giglamps, I'm safe to get through! — it's impossible for them to plough me, with all these contrivances. That's a consolation for a cove in distress, ain't it, old feller?'

Both our hero and Charles Larkyns endeavoured to persuade Mr. Bouncer that his conduct would, at the very least, be foolhardy, and that he had much better throw his pack of cards into the fire, wash the Kings of Israel and Judah off his shirt, destroy his strings and hooked wires, and keep his Examination-coat for a shooting one. But all their arguments were in vain, and the infatuated little gentleman, like a deaf adder, shut his ears at the voice of the charmer.

What between the Cowley cricketings, and the Isis boatings, Mr. Verdant Green only read by spasmodic fits; but, as he was very fairly up in his subjects — thanks to Charles Larkyns and the Rector — and as the Little-go was not such a very formidable affair, or demanded a scholar of first-rate calibre, the only terrors that the examination could bring him were those which were begotten of nervousness. At length the lists were out; and our hero read among the names of candidates, that of

'GREEN, *Verdant, e Coll. AEn. Fac.*'

There is a peculiar sensation on first seeing your name in print. Instances are on record where people have taken a world of trouble merely that they may have the pleasure of perusing their names 'among the fashionables present' at the Countess of So-and-so's evening-reception; and cases are not wanting where young ladies and gentlemen have expended no small amount of pocket-money in purchasing copies of *The Times* (no reduction, too, being made on taking a quantity!) in order that their sympathizing friends might have the pride of seeing their names as coming out at drawing-rooms and *levees*. When a young M.P. has stammered out his *coup-d'essai* in the House, he views, with mingled emotions, his name given to the world, for the first time, in capital letters. When young authors and artists first see their names in print, is it not a pleasure to them? When Ensign Dash sees himself gazetted, does he not look on his name with a peculiar sensation, and forthwith send an impression of the paper to Master Jones, who was flogged with him last week for stealing apples? When Mr. Smith is called to the Bar, and Mr. Robinson can dub himself M.R.C.S., do they not behold their names in print with feelings of rapture? And when Miss Brown has been to her first ball, does she not anxiously await the coming of the next county newspaper, in order to have the happiness of reading her name there?

But, different to these are the sensations that attend the seeing your name first in print in a College examination-list. They are, probably, somewhat similar to the sensations you would feel on seeing your name in a death-warrant. Your blood runs hot, then cold, then hot again; your pulse goes at fever pace; the throbbing arteries of your brow almost jerk your cap off. You know that the worst is come, — that the law of the Dons, which altereth not, has fixed your name there, and that there is no escape. The courage of despair then takes possession of your soul, and nerves you for the worst. You join the crowd of nervous fellow-sufferers who are thronging round the buttery-door to examine the list, and you begin with them calmly to parcel out the names by sixes and eights, and then to arrive at an opinion when your day of execution will be. If your name comes at the head of the list, you wish that you were 'YOUNG, *Carolus, e Coll. Vigorn.*' that you might have a reprieve of your sentence. If your name is at the end of the list, you wish that you were 'ADAMS, *Edvardus Jacobus,* e

Coll. Univ.' that you might go in at once, and be put out of your misery. If your name is in the middle of the list, you wish that it were elsewhere: and then you wish that it were out of the list altogether.

Through these varying shades of emotion did Mr. Verdant Green pass, until at length they were all lost in the deeper gloom of actual entrance into the schools. When once there, his fright soon passed away. Reassured by the kindly voice of the examiner, telling him to read over his Greek before construing it, our hero recovered his equanimity, and got through his *viva voce* with flying colours; and, on glancing over his paper-work, soon saw that the questions were within his scope, and that he could answer most of them. Without hazarding his success by making 'bad shots,' he contented himself by answering those questions only on which he felt sure; and, when his examination was over, he left the schools with a pretty safe conviction that he was safe, 'and was well through his smalls.'

He could not but help, however, feeling some anxiety on the subject, until he was relieved from all further fears, by the arrival of Messrs. Fosbrooke, Smalls, and Blades, with a slip of paper (not unlike those which Mr. Levi, the sheriff's officer, makes use of), on which was written and printed as follows: —

'GREEN, VERDANT, E COLL. AEN. FAC.
Quaestionibus Magistrorum Scholarum in Parviso pro forma respondit.

{GULIELMUS SMITH
Ita testamur {
{ROBERTUS JONES

Junii 7, 18 — .'

Alas for Mr. Bouncer! Though he had put in practice all the ingenious plans which were without a doubt to ensure his success; and though he had worked his cribs with consummate coolness, and had not been discovered; yet, nevertheless, his friends came to him empty-handed. The infatuated little gentleman had either trusted too much to his own astuteness, or else he had over-reached himself, and had used his card-knowledge in wrong places; or, perhaps, the examiners may have suspected his deeds from the nature of his papers, and may have refused to pass him. But whatever might be the cause, the little gentleman had to defer taking his degree for some months at least. In a word — and a dreadful word it is to all undergraduates — Mr. Bouncer was PLUCKED! He bore his unexpected reverse of fortune very philosophically, and professed to regret it only for 'the Mum's' sake; but he seemed to feel that the Dons of his college would look shy upon him, and he expressed his opinion that it would be better for him to migrate to the Tavern.

But, while Mr. Bouncer was thus deservedly punished for his idleness and duplicity, Charles Larkyns was rewarded for all his toil. He did even better than he had expected: for, not only did his name appear in the second class, but the following extra news concerning him was published in the daily papers, under the very appropriate heading of 'University *Intelligence*.'

> 'OXFORD, June 9. — The Chancellor's prizes have been awarded as follows: —
>
> 'Latin Essay, Charles Larkyns, Commoner of Brazenface. The Newdigate Prize for English Verse was also awarded to the same gentleman.'

His writing for the prize poem had been a secret. He had conceived the idea of doing so when the subject had been given out in the previous 'long:' he had worked at the subject privately, and, when the day (April 1) on which the poems had to be sent in, had come, he had watched his opportunity, and secretly dropped through the wired slit in the door of the registrar's office at the Clarendon, a manuscript poem, distinguished by the motto: —

> 'Oh for the touch of a vanish'd hand
> And the sound of a voice that is still.'

We may be quite sure that there was great rejoicing at the Manor Green and the Rectory, when the news arrived of the success of Charles Larkyns and Mr. Verdant Green.

12

Mr. Verdant Green and his Friends Enjoy the Commemoration

The Commemoration had come; and, among the people who were drawn to the sight from all parts of the country, the Warwickshire coach landed in Oxford our friends Mr. Green, his two eldest daughters, and the Rector — for all of whom Charles Larkyns had secured very comfortable lodgings in Oriel Street.

The weather was of the finest; and the beautiful city of colleges looked at its best. While the Rector met with old friends, and heard his son's praises, and renewed his acquaintance with his old haunts of study, Mr. Green again lionized Oxford in a much more comfortable and satisfactory manner than he had previously done at the heels of a professional guide. As for the young ladies, they were charmed with everything; for they had never before been in a University town, and all things had the fascination of novelty. Great were the luncheons held in Mr. Verdant

Green's and Charles Larkyns' rooms; musical was the laughter that floated merrily through the grave old quads of Brazenface; happy were the two hearts that held converse with each other in those cool cloisters and shady gardens. How a few flounces and bright girlish smiles can change the aspect of the sternest homes of knowledge! How sunlight can be brought into the gloomiest nooks of learning by the beams that irradiate happy girlish faces, where the light of love and truth shines out clear and joyous! How the appearance of the Commemoration week is influenced in a way thus described by one of Oxonia's poets: —

'Peace! for in the gay procession brighter
  forms are borne along —
Fairer scholars, pleasure-beaming, float
  amid the classic throng.
Blither laughter's ringing music fills the
  haunts of men awhile,
And the sternest priests of knowledge
  blush beneath a maiden's smile.
Maidens teach a softer science —
  laughing Love his pinions dips,
Hush'd to hear fantastic whispers
  murmur'd from a pedant's lips.
Oh, believe it, throbbing pulses flutter
  under folds of starch,

And the Dons are human-hearted if the
ladies' smiles be arch.'

Thanks to the influence of Charles Larkyns and his father, the party were enabled to see all that was to be seen during the Commemoration week. On the Saturday night they went to the amateur concert at the Town Hall, in aid of which, strange to say, Mr. Bouncer's proffer of his big drum had been declined. On the Sunday they went, in the morning, to St. Mary's to hear the Bampton lecture; and, in the afternoon, to the magnificent choral service at New College. In the evening they attended the customary 'Show Sunday' promenade in Christ Church Broad Walk, where, under the delicious cool of the luxuriant foliage, they met all the rank, beauty, and fashion that were assembled in Oxford; and where, until Tom 'tolled the hour for retiring,' they threaded their way amid a miscellaneous crowd of Dons and Doctors, and Tufts and Heads of Houses —

With prudes for Proctors, dowagers for Deans,

And bright girl-graduates with their golden hair.

On the Monday they had a party to Woodstock and Blenheim; and in the evening went, on the Brazenface barge, to see the procession of boats, where the Misses Green had the satisfaction to see their brother pulling in one of the fifteen torpids that followed immediately in the wake of the other boats. They concluded the evening's entertainments in a most satisfactory manner, by going to the ball at the Town Hall. Indeed, the way the two young ladies worked was worthy of all credit, and proved them to be possessed of the most vigorous constitutions; for, although they danced till an early hour in the morning, they not only, on the next day, went to the anniversary sermon for the Radcliffe, and after that to the horticultural show in the Botanical Gardens, and after that to the concert in the Sheldonian Theatre, but — as though they had not had enough to fatigue them already — they must, forsooth — Brazenface being one of the ball-giving colleges — wind up the night by accepting the polite invitation of Mr. Verdant Green and Mr. Charles Larkyns to a ball given in their college hall. And how many polkas these young ladies danced, and how many waltzes they waltzed, and how many ices they consumed, and how many too susceptible partners they drove to the verge of desperation, it would be improper, if not impossible, to say.

But, however much they might have been fagged by their exertions of feet and features, it is certain that, by ten of the clock the next morning, they appeared, quite fresh and charming to the view, in the ladies' gallery in the theatre. There — after the proceedings had been opened by the undergraduates in *their* peculiar way, and by the vice-chancellor in *his* peculiar way — and, after the degrees had been conferred, and the public orator had delivered an oration in a tongue not understanded of the people, our friends from Warwickshire had the delight of beholding Mr. Charles Larkyns ascend the rostrums to deliver, in their proper order, the Latin Essay and the English Verse. He had chosen his friend Verdant to be his prompter; so that the well-known 'Giglamps' of our hero formed, as it were, a very focus of attraction: but it was well for Mr. Charles Larkyns that he was possessed of self-control and a good memory, for Mr. Verdant Green was far too nervous to have prompted him in any efficient manner. We may be sure, that in all that bevy of fair women, at least one pair of bright eyes kindled with rapture, and one heart beat with exulting joy, when the deafening cheers that followed the poet's description of the moon, the sea, and woman's love (the three ingredients which are apparently necessary for the sweetening of all prize poems), rang through the theatre and made its walls re-echo to the shouting. And we may be sure that, when it was all over, and when the Commemoration had come to an end, Charles Larkyns felt rewarded for all his hours of labour by the deep love garnered up in his heart by the trustful affection of one who had become as dear to him as life itself!

It was one morning after they had all returned to the Manor Green that our hero said to his friend, 'How I *do* wish that this day week were come!'

'I dare say you do,' replied the friend: 'and I dare say that the pretty Patty is wishing the same wish.' Upon which Mr. Verdant Green not only laughed but blushed!

For it seemed that he, together with his sisters, Mr. Charles Larkyns, and Mr. Bouncer, were about to pay a long-vacation visit to Honeywood Hall, in the county of Northumberland; and the young man was naturally looking forward to it with all the ardour of a first and consuming passion.

Other titles published by Ulverscroft:

THE ADVENTURES OF MR. VERDANT GREEN

Cuthbert Bede

Young Mr. Verdant Green has tallied up eighteen years of unobjectionable existence at home with his sisters, comfortably insulated from the horrors of public school and the tyranny of sporting activities. But when Mr. Larkyns, local rector and Verdant's tutor, persuades Mr. Green Senior that his student is sorely in need of a little worldly experience, the callow Verdant is dispatched to Oxford for matriculation. As the innocent lamb embarks upon the odyssey of university life with characteristic trusting confidence, he finds himself gambolling into a den of wolves . . .

GREY GRANITE

Lewis Grassic Gibbon

Widowed once again, Chris Colquohon has come to the industrial town of Duncairn, where life is as hard as the granite of the buildings all around her, and she must make her living as best she can by working in Ma Cleghorn's boarding house. Meanwhile, her son Ewan, forsaking his college career, finds employment at a steel manufacturer's, and determines to lead a peaceful strike against the manufacture of armaments. In the face of violence and police brutality, his socialist idealism is forged into something harder and fiercer as he readies himself to sacrifice all for the cause . . .

A TANGLED WEB

L. M. Montgomery

It all begins with Great Aunt Becky and her infamous prized possession: a legendary heirloom jug. After her death, everyone wants it. But the name of the new owner will not be revealed for one year . . . Over the next twelve months, scandals, quarrels and love affairs abound within the Dark and Penhallow clans — with the jug at the centre of it all. Engagements are broken; lifelong mutual hatred blossoms into romance; lovers separated years ago are reunited. But then comes the night that the eccentric matriarch's wishes will be revealed — and both families are in for the biggest surprise of them all.

VICE VERSA

F. Anstey

Mr. Bultitude is unmoved by the pleading of his fourteen-year-old son Dick that he be spared from returning to Grimstone's tortuous boarding school. During his harangue on the free and easy life of youth, Mr. Bultitude unwisely expresses the wish that he himself might be a boy again — whilst clutching the magical Garudâ Stone, which is all too ready to oblige by transforming his outward appearance into that of his son's. To add insult to injury, Dick swiftly seizes the stone — and with it, the opportunity not only to assume his father's mature and portly form, but also gleefully pack Mr. Bultitude off to the hellish halls of Grimstone's . . .

THE AWAKENING

Kate Chopin

The Pontellier family are spending a hot, lazy holiday on the Gulf of Mexico. Nobody expects that Edna should be preoccupied with anything more than her husband Léonce and their small boys. But Edna, restive and achieving fulfilment only in her beloved sketching, finds her allocated bonds of motherhood and wifely duty to be stifling constraints. And when she teeters on the brink of an illicit summer romance with young clerk Robert Lebrun, new ideas and longings are awakened in her . . .

THE HAUNTED HOUSE

Charles Dickens & Hesba Stretton

In 1859, various literary luminaries — including Charles Dickens, Elizabeth Gaskell and Wilkie Collins — collaborated on a serialised work concerning events in a most peculiar house. This is their tale . . . When our narrator espies a deserted house from his railway carriage, he cannot resist the challenge of taking up residence in a place no one else will inhabit. Local legend has terrified the nearby villagers, who in turn convince his servants to abandon ship. Undaunted, he and his sister invite a group of friends to join them — each of whom is then commissioned to rout out the supernatural from their respective rooms. And come Twelfth Night, they will meet to recount their experiences . . .